D1049962

Above and Beyond

BY THE SAME AUTHOR

The Silver Balloon

Edwina Victorious

SUSAN BONNERS

Above and Beyond

CHATTAHOOCHEE VALLEY LIBRARIES

NEW YORK

Copyright © 2001 by Susan Bonners
All rights reserved
Distributed in Canada by Douglas & McIntyre Ltd.
Printed in the United States of America
Designed by Vincenzo Longo
First edition, 2001
1 3 5 7 9 10 8 6 4 2

Library of Congress Cataloging-in-Publication Data
Bonners, Susan.
    Above and beyond / Susan Bonners.
        p. cm.
    Summary: Jerry befriends the class clown Danny and discovers
disturbing secrets from the past.
    ISBN 0-374-30018-6
    [1. Friendship—Fiction.] I. Title.

PZ7.B64253 Ab 2001
[Fic]—dc21

                                                    00-68157

To Barry—for the word "sure,"
and for never failing to say it in response to
"Can we talk about my story? Just read it from here . . ."

CONTENTS

Above and Beyond

The Wisecrack King

Jerry Wheelock glanced at the clock. Ten minutes to go in social studies class before the Friday lunch bell. Mrs. Finneran was talking about the importance of point of view in writing history, using Christopher Columbus's voyages as an example.

"What is the implication behind the words 'Columbus discovered America'? Anyone? I know it's the end of May, but you'll have to fight off spring fever for a few more weeks. Yes, Patricia, what does that statement mean to you?"

"That he was the first person to get here."

"How would you rephrase that statement to make it more accurate?"

Before Patricia could answer, Danny Casey spoke

up. "I'd say he made the world's most unsuccessful trip for Chinese takeout."

A ripple of laughter passed through the room. Since his transfer in April from Jefferson, the other district school, Danny had been a nonstop source for wisecracks. Sometimes Jerry thought they were funny, but other times, like now, he wished Danny would stop interrupting everybody.

"Danny," said Mrs. Finneran, "I don't want to have to tell you again to raise your hand. Speaking out of turn is unfair to the other students. Patricia?"

"He was the first European to discover it."

"Of course," said Mrs. Finneran, "we have some evidence that explorers from the Scandinavian countries landed in present-day Canada, but you've got the idea. Why do so many history books say that Columbus discovered America?"

Danny waved his hand wildly.

"Yes, Danny?"

"The Indians didn't have an agent," said Danny.

"You're making a joke as usual, but there's a grain of truth in what you said. What does an agent do that might apply here? Come on, Danny, think."

"An agent would have gotten the Indians a better deal," said Danny.

"What would a better deal have been?"

"A cut of the profits from Columbus Day sales."

Mrs. Finneran shook her head. "You've got a good mind, Danny. I wish you'd use it for something besides making jokes. Please stay and see me when the lunch bell rings." She pointed to the second row. "Robert, I think I saw your hand up."

"Nobody spoke up for the Indians or asked them to write a history book."

"Exactly. Until recently, Native Americans didn't have much chance to tell the story from their point of view. As an example, I'm going to read you a passage from a history text used in schools when I was your age."

Just then, the bell rang. "We'll start from here next time," Mrs. Finneran said.

Jerry picked up his books and headed for his locker. In the hallway, he caught up with his best friends, Phil Clark, Eddie Matthews, and Tom Everett.

"Looks like the Wisecrack King is going to Mr. Harrison's office again," said Phil.

"By now, he must have a chair with his name on it," said Eddie. "You'd think he'd knock it off when he sees Mrs. Finneran's really had it."

"I don't think he sees it," said Tom.

"That's impossible," said Phil. "Everybody else does. Although he is pretty weird. Like last Saturday, a few of us are playing a pickup soccer game in Edison Park when Danny comes by. The ball goes out of bounds. He starts dribbling it like he's in the game.

"Which reminds me, Jerry, next time it's your turn to be soccer captain in gym, don't pick him to be on our team again. He hogs the ball."

"He scored points, though," said Jerry. "We won that game."

"Other guys could have scored those points if he hadn't been hotdogging," said Eddie. "He won't pass the ball and that cost us points."

"Yeah," said Phil, "he doesn't get it that he's on a team. And he's a pain. I mean, he's funny and all, but I'm tired of listening to him brag—like how he was the best soccer player at Jefferson."

"How come he got transferred in April anyway?" said Eddie.

Eric Thorpe walked up. "Because Mr. Harrison got more money for that after-school program he's in. You know, the one where they try to teach misfits how to act normal. I know because my aunt's on the school board. And I might know some other things about him, but I don't want to say anything—since he's your teammate and all. Bye." He disappeared into the crowd.

"What do you suppose he knows?" said Eddie.

"Probably nothing," said Jerry. "He just likes to give us a hard time."

Late the next morning, Jerry pedaled his new mountain bike out of the garage and took a left at the end of the driveway. Two blocks down Sycamore Street, he reached the first hill. Grasping the shift lever, he searched for first gear. With a clash of metal on metal, the bike ground to a halt. Jerry looked at the rear wheel. The chain had come off its sprocket. Would he ever get the hang of shifting? He got off the bike and fumbled with the greasy chain.

"Hi! Need help?"

Jerry glanced up in the direction of the voice.

Danny Casey was coming down the street. Jerry was not in the mood for wisecracks just now, especially at his expense.

"No, I can take care of it, thanks."

He struggled with the mechanism a few minutes more, but he had no idea what to do.

"Do you know how the chain goes back on?" he said at last.

"I bet I can figure it out." Danny sounded completely confident. He began tinkering with the chain. Jerry watched nervously.

"I've got a manual in our garage that shows how the gears work," Jerry said. "Maybe we'd better check it."

Danny fiddled a half minute more. "Sounds good."

"It's the blue house on the corner." Jerry turned the bike around and they started down Sycamore. "I didn't know you lived around here, Danny."

"I don't," he said. "I had to get some rawhide chews for my dog at the pet store, and I decided to take the scenic route back. These houses are really something else." He pointed to the Shaws' two-car garage. "You could fit my whole house in there."

Jerry had never thought of the homes as especially big. "Did you know I lived here?"

"Sort of," said Danny. "I heard your friend Phil tell Eddie about a fender bender right in front of your house on Sycamore Street."

"That was last week," said Jerry. He wondered if Danny had been looking for his house.

In the Wheelocks' driveway, Jerry set the bike on its kickstand and swung open the garage door. The manual was on the workbench. He flipped through it.

"Here," he said, handing it over. "Read it starting with 'Troubleshooting the Gears.' "

Danny glanced over the page several times. From the way his eyes moved, Jerry could tell he wasn't reading. Maybe what he'd heard was true—that Danny could barely read. He started to take back the manual. "Maybe I should read this stuff out loud while you—"

Danny turned to the next page. A series of diagrams was featured.

"Now we're talking," he said. He focused on the drawings. Then he handed the manual back and sat down next to the bike.

Jerry found the Table of Contents. "Maybe we should go over the part on shifting. Let's see. 'Adjusting the pedals and handlebars . . . tire pressure . . . braking . . .'"

"Done!" said Danny. The chain was back in place. "Got a rag or something?"

Jerry handed him a towel from the workbench, then took the bike for a trial spin around the driveway. "How did you know which sprockets to put the chain on?" he said, setting the bike on the kickstand again.

"Simple. You've got to get it in line with that thing." Danny pointed to a device below the sprockets.

Jerry found the diagram. "The 'derailleur.'"

"If you say so. Anyway, just follow the picture. You're better off with a bike like mine. One gear. No shifting." He tossed the towel back on the bench and saw the warranty card that Jerry had filled out for the bike.

"Jeremiah Wheelock. Is that your real name?"

Jerry nodded. This was a fact he didn't generally advertise. "My father's father was Jeremiah. You get named after your grandfather in my family. Was anybody in your family a Daniel?"

"Not that I know. Besides, my name is just Danny. I heard that my dad always liked the song 'Danny Boy.' He was probably singing it in some bar the night I was born."

The way Danny talked about him, Jerry wondered if his father had died, but he didn't want to ask.

The front door of the house opened. Two men came down the steps, Jerry's older cousin Charles followed by Jerry's father.

"I'll keep you posted, Cal," said Charles, "unless the town council has me shipped to parts unknown. While I was making my pitch for that Center Street pedestrian mall, I was sure Regina Elliott was going to skewer me with her hatpin."

"The council isn't exactly a hotbed of revolution- ary thinking," said Jerry's father. "It's times like this I remember why I went in for civil engineering. Sur- veying instruments are so much easier to deal with than any committee I've ever been on."

"Next time," said Charles, "your wife has to be there. Margaret's the only member of the council who can take on Regina, hatpin and all." He turned toward the driveway. "Jerry! How are you?"

When other people asked that, Jerry felt they were being polite. Charles really wanted to know.

"Fine. I had a little bike trouble, but Danny and I figured it out. Mostly, Danny did. Oh. This is Danny Casey. Danny, this is my dad and my cousin Charles Findlay."

Charles came over and shook Danny's hand. "Trouble with the gears?" He could have been talking to another adult, someone who had interesting things to say.

"The chain slipped," said Danny, falling into Charles's matter-of-fact tone, "but it's fixed now."

"Good job. Jer, how did that science project go?"

"Really well, thanks to Nate."

Charles turned to Danny. "Nate's the smart cousin. The rest of us are just good-looking."

"Speak for yourself," said Jerry's father. "As Margaret will be happy to tell you, she's smart and good-looking."

Charles laughed. "Indeed she is." He waved as he started down the walk. "So long, guys. Nice meeting you, Danny."

"Good luck on the project, Charles," Jerry's father called after him. "If you can deal with Regina Elliott, you'll deserve another medal for valor." He started up the steps. "Jerry, I have to make a phone call. Then I want to take a look at that bike. It may need a little adjustment. Leave it in the garage." He waved and went back inside.

"Did you say that was your cousin?" said Danny, watching as Charles's car went down the street. "He's about the same age as your dad, isn't he?"

"He's my mother's cousin. That means he's my first cousin once removed."

"Removed?"

"You need a diagram to understand it."

"What did your father mean about 'another medal for valor'?"

"Charles was a medic in Vietnam. He got the Silver Star. He exposed himself to heavy fire," said Jerry, remembering the words of the citation, "without regard for his own safety. I'm not sure exactly what he did, but he saved the lives of three men. It was one of those 'above and beyond the call of duty' things. He got shot himself, so he's got a Purple Heart, too."

Danny whistled. "He seemed like somebody important. And he's on the council?"

"He's head of the town planning board."

Danny retrieved his bag of rawhide chews. "Let's go check out Sid's Comics and see if he's got any new stuff."

Jerry hadn't planned on spending any time with Danny, but he couldn't think of a way out of it. He went up the steps and called through the screen door. "We're going downtown." His father nodded without interrupting his phone conversation.

Jerry left his bike by the workbench and pulled down the garage door. So much for a fun Saturday pedaling around the neighborhood.

"You know Sid's, right?" said Danny as they started back up the street.

Jerry shook his head. "Why don't we go to McGrath's Comics? I go there a lot."

Danny made a face. "Forget McGrath's. My place is a whole lot better. You'll see."

They walked the three blocks to Bridgewater Avenue and took a right. The sidewalk was crowded with shoppers. Danny stopped to look at a window display. Jerry went on ahead. Then he heard his name called. When he turned around, Phil, Eddie, and Tom were coming up on their bicycles.

"Jerry," said Phil, pulling alongside, "we went by your house. We're going to KaZam Video. Want to come?"

Danny appeared at Jerry's side. Jerry caught the glances exchanged by his friends.

"Jerry and me have plans," said Danny. "Right, Jerry?" Jerry looked at Phil, then at Danny. "Right, Jerry?" Danny said again.

"Maybe tomorrow, Phil," said Jerry. "See you." He felt Danny's hand on his arm, steering him down the sidewalk. Behind them, he heard Phil say in an undertone, "That's what you get for being a nice guy." If Danny heard the remark, he gave no sign.

They walked a long way on Bridgewater, farther than Jerry had ever gone on foot, past the lumberyard where he and his father sometimes shopped on Saturdays, past the appliance warehouse, past the cement plant.

"We're going to Sid's, aren't we?" said Jerry.

"Sure, but there's this other place you've got to see. They just opened up. It's only a couple of blocks out of the way."

Six blocks later, just after the railroad crossing, Danny pointed to a stucco building with a sign that read "Tropical World."

Once past the inner door, Jerry found himself in a dim cavernous space, the only illumination provided by row after row of lighted aquariums.

"These are mostly saltwater," said Danny. "A whole lot more interesting than freshwater."

Jerry followed Danny past tanks of dazzling tropical fish and creatures he'd seen only at the Aquarium—sea horses, shrimp, anemones, starfish. One tank even contained a tiny octopus.

When they finally stepped outside into the brilliant sunshine again, Jerry felt like a deep-sea diver resurfacing.

"That was fantastic," he said.

"Told you. Now we'll get something to eat at the Acropolis Bakery. It's right near here."

By then, Jerry had an idea of what "right near here" might mean. They left Bridgewater Avenue and went down a series of side streets. Jerry lost track of what direction they were going. At last he saw the Acropolis, sandwiched in between a pawnshop and a secondhand furniture store.

Inside, a group of elderly men sat in a cluster around a wooden table. Jerry was about to ask Danny what language they were speaking when he made the connection—the Acropolis was in Greece. The glass case was full of baked goods that Jerry had never seen before. He turned to the hand-lettered price list. He couldn't read a single word. Why didn't they have a price list in English for their customers who didn't know Greek?

When the young woman ahead of them began giving her order, Jerry realized he and Danny were the only customers who didn't know Greek.

When their turn came, Danny pointed to a tray. "Two of these."

"Two-fifty," said the woman behind the counter.

"Let me get it," said Jerry, reaching into his pocket, "for fixing my bike."

Danny gestured toward a tiny table. "Sit over there."

The table wobbled and the chair felt as if it would collapse any second. Cautiously, Jerry bit into the triangle of pastry Danny set in front of him. He found himself with a mouthful of flakes oozing with honey. Before long, flakes were stuck to his nose,

his chin, his sleeves. His fingers were glued together.

"What is it?"

"Baklava. It'll double your cavities, but it's worth
it."

Jerry nodded. They left the Acropolis still licking
honey off their fingers.

"We'll take the shortcut to Sid's," Danny said.

Did Danny ever ask his friends what they wanted to
do? Jerry felt as if he'd been kidnapped. All the same,
he was interested to see where they would go next.

The "shortcut" went through a maze of streets and
litter-strewn alleys. The ramshackle wood frame build-
ings seemed to lean on one another for support.
They passed a sign, "Artistic Tattoo, One Flight Up."

"My Uncle Jack has a tattoo," said Danny, "a cougar.
I'm going to get one as soon as I save up the money."

"Don't you need to be eighteen?"

"All you need is a piece of paper that says you are.
Nobody checks."

Sid's was in the middle of the block. Danny
reached for the doorknob. "Thanks to me, you're
about to discover the mother lode."

Jerry thought Danny was bragging again until he

walked in. From behind stacks of comic books came a muffled voice. "Hi, Danny. Who's your friend?"

"Hi, Sid. This is Jerry Wheelock."

"Hi," Jerry said, still unable to see anyone.

"Got any new stuff?" said Danny.

Sid emerged from his fortress. "First two racks on the left," he said.

While Danny went through the racks, Jerry walked up and down the aisles. Adventure, sci-fi, horror, superheroes, and cowboys—Sid had it all in massive amounts. Jerry wondered why he and his friends thought McGrath's was so great.

He explored the sci-fi and adventure sections. Then he moved on to the Tales of the Undead bin. *The Corpse That Wouldn't Stay Buried* was up front, the cover featuring a creepy cemetery full of grotesque monuments.

Cemetery. Suddenly Jerry remembered he'd promised to help his mother fix up family graves that afternoon. She was closing her garden supply shop early to make time. She'd be busy at the shop tomorrow and Monday since this was the Memorial Day weekend and lots of people would be buying flowering plants to put on graves.

He checked his watch. "Danny, I have to go home. I promised to help my mom weed family plots at the cemetery."

Danny looked baffled. "What's the hurry? Believe me, Jerry, those relatives you've got in the cemetery— they're really removed. They don't notice the weeds."

"My mom does. Anyway, I promised."

Danny seemed to deflate. "Well, you don't want to keep those dead people waiting. You can get a bus on Montclare."

"Um, that's a couple of blocks up the hill, right?"

Danny seemed surprised. "No, it's the other way. I guess you don't know the streets around here. I'll walk you."

At Montclare, Jerry saw a bus coming. He ran to catch the green light.

"Maybe we can get together next week," he yelled from across the street. "I'd like to go back to Sid's."

"Okay!" Danny yelled as the bus pulled up.

Jerry found a seat and waved to Danny from the window. Danny was still standing on the corner as the bus pulled away. Jerry wondered if he would go back to Sid's by himself. Then he looked at his watch again.

On the ride back home, he thought about the unexpected turns his day had taken. He was glad he had agreed to go with Danny.

Jerry got off the bus at Madison Street and ran the five blocks to his house. His mother was loading flats of little plants into the trunk of her car when he jogged into the driveway, gasping for breath.

"We're trying to honor our deceased ancestors, Jerry, not join them. You'd better rest a minute." She picked up a box of garden tools. "Why don't you get in the car? This is the last of it."

Jerry got in the front seat. His mother slipped behind the wheel and started the engine. "Are my eyes going or was that your father I saw zipping down Sycamore on your new bike about a half hour ago?"

Jerry explained about the gears needing adjusting.

"How was your day?" his mother asked.

"Fine. I ran into somebody from school."

"Who was that?"

"Danny Casey."

"Casey . . . Casey . . . Do I know the family?"

"I don't think so."

"Your father probably does, now that he's on the school board. What did you do?"

"Oh, just messed around." Jerry decided not to mention exactly where he'd been. He'd never gone that far without permission.

At Briarwood Cemetery, they parked on a gravel road and lugged the supplies to the headstone of Agnes Bennett Findlay, Jerry's great-grandmother.

Rain had fallen the night before, so digging in the soil was easy. Jerry liked to watch his mother garden. She worked with no wasted motion, completely at home with her hands in the dirt.

"Mom, Agnes was Nate's great-grandmother, too, wasn't she?"

"Yes."

She was also Charles Findlay's grandmother, but Jerry could never keep it straight. His mother understood about second cousins and third cousins and "once removed" and "twice removed." But her attitude toward the intricate web of family connections was a mystery. Sometimes she made fun of anybody who took the subject seriously.

"Some people around here," she had said more than once, "think you need at least three generations of illustrious ancestors planted in Briarwood or you don't count."

All the same, she cared in some way, enough to spend time putting flowers on the graves, even the ones of long-dead relatives she never knew.

"Let's go there next," she said, pointing to the headstone of Phillip Farnsworth, her father's father.

The Farnsworths could muster only a small contingent, flanked on two sides by Findlays. Meanwhile, on a nearby hill, the Wheelocks seemed to have staked out the high ground early, led by Caleb Wheelock, Jerry's great-grandfather on his father's side.

They worked on his grave last. When they finished, Jerry's mother sat on her heels and stretched.

"Time to go home. We're out of flowers, and I think I'm out of steam."

They threaded their way back to the car, past Bennetts and Shaws and Aldriches and Everetts. Jerry had never seen any Caseys in Briarwood. If Danny's father was dead, he must be buried somewhere else.

Nobody's Fool

Jerry slouched at his desk as Eric Thorpe brought the class discussion—family stories as history—around to his favorite subject, the accomplishments of Stanton Thorpe. Everyone in class, except for Danny, had heard about Eric's grandfather more than once.

"—and after two terms as mayor and one as chairman of the town council, he was named president of Whitmore College, then chancellor. But he gave that up when he was elected to a judgeship."

"Sounds like he couldn't keep a steady job," said Danny.

Giggles broke out. Mrs. Finneran gave Danny a warning glance. "Please continue, Eric."

"And that," Eric said, looking daggers at Danny, "is why it's called Stanton Thorpe Square."

"Oh," said Danny innocently, "I thought that 'square' was a description of him."

"Now everybody settle down," said Mrs. Finneran, raising her voice above the laughter. "Besides family stories, what's another way we get information about the past?"

"Newspapers," said Amanda Aldrich.

"Good. Even very old newspapers and magazines are often available on microfilm. What's another way?"

"Talking to eyewitnesses," said Eric. "My great-uncle Everett Thorpe was president of Colonial Bank and Trust on Sayer Street. He witnessed the stock market crash."

"Witnessed it?" said Danny. "I thought he started it."

Laughter erupted again. Even Pamela Woodword, the best-behaved girl in class, was giggling.

"Danny, the next interruption means a trip to Mr. Harrison's office," said Mrs. Finneran. "Yes, Eric, personal accounts are valuable."

"Archaeology," said Pamela.

"Yes," said Mrs. Finneran. "Sometimes you can literally dig up the past. Now that you've got the idea, I want each of you to write a report—about two or three pages—on some event that happened in our local area before you were born. It doesn't have to be something big and important. It could be something you heard as a family story. If you have trouble finding a topic, I have a list of suggestions.

"Do some brainstorming. Try to come up with more than one source for information about the event. The reports are due in three weeks, on Tuesday, June 22."

A groan went through the class.

"You haven't heard the good part yet," said Mrs. Finneran with a twinkle in her eye. "At the end-of-term awards ceremony on the evening of June 25, you will read your reports aloud to your classmates and parents."

The bell rang for lunch. In the cafeteria, Jerry got in line behind Phil, Tom, and Eddie.

"So, Jerry," said Phil, "how was your afternoon with Mr. Wonderful?"

"Yeah, Jerry," said Tom, "where'd you go?"

Instead of answering right away, Jerry sorted

through the sandwiches and put one on his tray. He wasn't eager to talk about his day with Danny. In reciting the facts, he might lose the sense of having been on an adventure. "Oh, a few places Danny knows."

"Like where?" said Phil, reaching for a cheeseburger.

"Well, we went to a place that sells tropical fish."

"Jerry, you can see tropical fish at Petland."

"Not like this. The place has saltwater setups. It was pretty terrific."

"Where is it?" said Eddie.

"Past the railroad crossing on Bridgewater."

"How'd you get out there?" said Tom.

"We walked."

"Are you kidding?" said Phil. "That's about four miles. I told you this guy's weird."

"Where'd you go after that?" said Eddie.

"We got something to eat." At that moment, Danny appeared at the door of the cafeteria. He scanned the room, then walked straight to Jerry.

"Hey, Jer, let's sit together." He didn't seem to notice that Jerry was with his friends.

"We always sit at the same table," said Phil. "It's kind of full just now. Sorry."

"Come on, Phil," said Eddie, grabbing a sandwich and heading down the first aisle. "It's already ten after."

Jerry didn't want to leave Danny by himself, but he was irritated to be stuck in the middle like this.

Danny checked the sandwich on Jerry's tray. "Baloney? Boring." He put it back. "There's got to be something else. Let's see. 'Avocado salad.' Do you know what that is?"

"No."

"Neither do I," said Danny. He took two avocado salad sandwich rolls and tossed one on Jerry's tray and one on his, then added two apples and two cartons of orange juice. "I guess that's it. Got everything you wanted?"

Jerry wondered if Danny meant to be funny.

They found seats together. Jerry took the plastic off his sandwich.

"Are those green chunks the avocado?" said Danny.

"I guess." Jerry took a small bite, preparing to wash it down with a gulp of orange juice. To his surprise, he liked it. He took a big bite.

"Do I know what I'm doing or what?" said Danny. "So what are you going to do your report on?"

"I don't know."

"Why not write about your cousin who got the medals? He must have some good war stories."

"That's an idea. Wait. The event has to be something that happened around here, not in Vietnam."

"Right. I forgot."

But the mention of Charles reminded Jerry of something.

"Charles did something else I could write about. He rescued a little girl. She got lost in the woods above Miller's Creek and fell from a cliff. She landed on a ledge. Charles was a rock climber. He got her off the ledge. My mom says it was in the papers. There's even a plaque on the cliff where it happened. He was only eighteen."

"That's lucky. You've got the answer right there."

"Did anybody in your family ever do anything interesting?" said Jerry.

"Not that Mrs. Finneran would want me to put in a report. I guess I'll have to throw myself on her mercy—what's left of it."

"You could try keeping quiet. Those cracks are getting you in trouble."

"I know, but I can't help it. My mouth's on autopilot."

On the way home from school that day, Jerry stopped at the public library. He explained to Mrs. Tracy, the reference librarian, what he was looking for.

"Well, if you don't have a specific date, you'll have to look through a lot of microfilm to find the right copy of the *Courier*. A small newspaper like that doesn't have an index."

Jerry's mother would know. He could come back tomorrow. He was about to leave when he remembered the plaque. He'd seen it about a year ago when he and his father went hiking. The date was on it. He wrote it on a call slip and gave it to Mrs. Tracy.

"I'll be right back," she said.

Minutes later, Jerry was sitting at a microfilm reader, turning the crank, as Mrs. Tracy had shown him. As he wound the film from the spool onto the take-up reel, pages of the *Courier* flew past in a blur. January, February, March. He felt as if he were at the controls of a time machine. April, May, June.

He applied the brakes. July 5. July 17. July 26, page 1.

The banner headline read: "Jennifer's Safe!" The subhead continued the story: "Rock-Climbing Teen Rescues Girl from Ledge."

Jerry adjusted the focus and began to read.

FEATURE TO THE *COURIER* BY ROBERT DAVIS. *Anyone who wrings his hands over the state of American youth should meet Charles Findlay. He's a soft-spoken eighteen-year-old who graduated high school with honors last June, works a full-time job, and volunteers with the local literacy program. Last spring, he took up rock climbing. Yesterday evening, he saved the life of a little girl.*

Charles was on his way to work yesterday morning when he heard on the radio that five-year-old Jennifer Atwood had been reported missing. She was believed to have wandered into the woods that border the Atwoods' property.

When she hadn't been found by five o'clock, Charles decided to join the search party, based at Chandler's Lodge. And he did one more thing: he stopped at home to get his climbing gear.

Light rain began falling as he parked at the trail-head. A ten-minute hike took him to the top of Eagle Bluff, two hundred feet above Miller's Creek. He was about to start down the far side when he heard a mewing sound—an animal, he thought. Then he realized he was hearing the crying of a child. He crept to the edge of the bluff and peered down.

Thirty feet below, on a narrow ledge, Jennifer was lying on her side with her back against the rockface. As Charles watched in horror, she moved her foot, causing a loose section of rock to break off the ledge and go tumbling into the valley. Fearful of causing her to move again, he didn't dare call to her.

Charles was faced with an agonizing decision. Should he leave Jennifer and try to find the other searchers, knowing that she might fall to her death before a rescue could be mounted? Or should he try to bring her up himself? Charles stepped into his harness.

He knew this bluff. He'd descended it before using a stout tree near the edge as an anchor point. It would be his fail-safe if he fell on the climb back up. He clipped a short rope to his belt and passed a longer one around the tree, doubling the rope back on itself.

Charles slung this doubled rope over one shoulder and under one leg, then let it glide through his hands as he backed down the cliff in the controlled slide known as rappelling.

In seconds, he was at the ledge. Charles found a foothold and tied off his rope, freeing his hands.

He did his best to calm Jennifer as he unclipped the short rope from his belt and looped it into a harness for her. With tears still streaming down her face, Jennifer struggled into it. Charles knotted her harness to his, then shifted her to his back.

Eagle Bluff is nearly a vertical drop at that point. Charles needed every handhold in the climber's repertory as he grappled back up. On the way, he "tied off" several times, a technique of knotting the trailing rope to limit a fall.

When they got to the top, Jennifer was shivering violently. Charles slipped off their harnesses, found his discarded jacket, and draped it over her. Then he picked her up and started down the path to Chandler's Lodge.

By the time he met up with the main search party twenty minutes later, she had fallen asleep in his arms.

Jerry put a coin in the machine and pressed "Copy," then "Rewind." He had heard about the rescue before—not from Charles, he never talked about it, or about his experiences in the war either. But the story circulated in the family, and Jerry had heard parts of it at different times. This was the first time the whole picture had come together.

He put the copy in his pocket, slipped the microfilm spool into its box, and returned it to Mrs. Tracy. As he pushed open the main door, the afternoon sunlight was a shock. In his mind, he was still at the top of Eagle Bluff.

Crossing Bridgewater Avenue, he saw Danny standing in front of McGrath's Comics. Jerry walked up to the display window. Danny was looking at a cover illustration featuring a dark-haired man in camouflage gear.

"Hi, Danny. You're done with your after-school program? Want to go inside?"

Before he could answer, Eric Thorpe and one of his friends came around the corner.

"It's Mr. Big Mouth," said Eric. "So what great things did your relatives do?"

Danny shrugged. "Not much."

"That's not what I hear," said Eric, stepping close to Danny, who was several inches shorter. "I hear that your uncle went to prison. Twice."

Danny looked steadily at Eric for a few seconds. He smiled pleasantly. "I hear that nobody in your family gets past the city limits. Ever."

Eric blinked in confusion. He started to say something, then stopped.

"Come on, Jerry," said Danny. "Eric needs time to think." He turned around and started down Sayer Street. Jerry caught up with him and fell into step.

Behind them, Jerry heard Eric say, "I'll bet you think that was clever."

They kept on walking. Neither of them said anything until they got to the middle of the block.

"My uncle knows his way around lots of places," Danny said at last. "He even lived in Mexico for a while."

"Did he really spend time in prison?" Jerry had never known anybody with relatives who'd served time in prison.

"He's there now."

"Is he your dad's brother?"

"My mom's. His name is Jack Maguire, but everybody calls him Blackjack. He's nobody's fool, you know? The first time he went to prison, the cops just got lucky. The car he stole had a taillight out and he got pulled over for it."

"Do you remember that?"

"No, that was before I was born. And they only caught him the second time because somebody ratted. Otherwise, they never would have caught him."

"Who ratted?" Jerry tried to sound offhand like Danny.

"The other guy who hijacked the Wells Fargo truck with him. He was so dumb, he got caught."

"Do you ever visit him?"

Danny didn't answer right away. "See, the prison isn't around here."

"So you haven't seen him for a long time?"

"Not since I was four. He'd been in a year for the Wells Fargo job by then, but they let him out for a day so he could go to my grandma's funeral. A guard came with him. Of course, he could have gotten away if he'd wanted to. In a couple of years I'll be able to go places on my own. I'll go see him whenever I want."

"Doesn't your mother want to see him?" As soon as he'd blurted out the question, Jerry was sorry.

After an uncomfortable silence, Danny said, "She's kind of angry."

Jerry wondered how he would feel having an Uncle Jack Maguire instead of an Uncle Phillip Farnsworth and an Uncle Barnett Wheelock. People expected a lot of you when you were both a Farnsworth and a Wheelock. Maybe Danny was lucky.

"We'll go to my house," said Danny. "You can stay for supper. My mom won't mind. She'll be home from work about five-thirty."

"Well, I can come for a little while, but I have to be home for supper."

"You're sure?"

"I'm sure."

"Okay. It's only a few blocks."

Like the shortcut to Sid's, the walk was longer than a few blocks and took Jerry into a neighborhood he'd never been in, rows of small frame houses with sagging porches. Dogs barked at them from behind chain-link fences. All the same, Jerry was interested to see what was on these streets. Strange that he'd never thought to come here himself.

Danny's house was like the others, but more cheerful. Petunias streamed out of the window boxes. In the front yard, an old truck tire had been cut into a planter for more flowers. From inside the house, Jerry heard barking.

"That's Blackie," Danny said.

Blackie sounded like a big dog to Jerry. "Maybe we should stay in the yard," he said.

"Blackie won't hurt you," said Danny, pulling out his key, "except he might drown you in slobber."

He opened the door a few inches. A rangy long-haired dog pounced on him and began enthusiastically licking his face. "Cut it out!" Danny screwed up his face and tried to turn away, but he was laughing. "Save some of that for Jerry." He pushed his way inside.

"I'd better call my mom so she won't be worried," Jerry said.

Danny pointed to the phone on an end table in the living room and went into the kitchen with Blackie dancing circles around him.

"I've got to take Blackie out," he called. "Back in a minute." Jerry heard the screen door open and close.

He dialed the shop. His mother answered.

"The Uptown Gardener."

"Mom, it's me. I'm at Danny Casey's house. I'll be home before supper, okay?"

"No later than six, Jerry."

"Okay."

"Where does Danny live?"

"On Howell Street."

There was a short silence.

"I'll have your father pick you up on his way home. What's the address?"

"Just a sec." With his free hand, Jerry opened the front door and looked at the number. "Thirty-nine," he said, closing it again.

"Okay. Be outside at six-ten. Bye!"

Jerry sat down on the sofa and found himself being slowly engulfed by the puffy, threadbare cushions. Opposite him, the worn armchair was covered with an afghan. A beat-up piano stood against one wall.

A few framed photographs were set on the end

tables. Two of them were of Danny and somebody who had to be his mother. Another one was probably Danny with his grandmother. Jerry didn't see any photos that might show Danny's father or his uncle.

Maybe they had family albums someplace. Jerry's mother kept a whole shelf of albums and a portrait gallery besides. It covered an entire living-room wall and was spreading like ivy over the mantel and up the staircase.

Jerry decided that he liked this sofa. It reminded him of an enormous marshmallow. The back door opened. Jerry heard the whirr of a can opener, then the sound of food being gulped.

A minute later, Blackie trotted in and jumped into the armchair. Danny slid in beside him.

"Does your mom let Blackie on the furniture?"

"Sure," said Danny. He seemed puzzled by the question.

"What kind of dog is he?"

"He's a curbstone setter," said Danny.

"I never heard of that breed."

Danny laughed. "That means he's a mutt. I found him in a vacant lot. He was in bad shape. His ribs were sticking out and he had fleas and stuff. My mom almost had a fit when I brought him home.

"But I fixed him up. We took him to a vet. I got all kinds of medicine to give him and shampoo to kill the fleas. Now he looks like a champ."

With his long silky coat, Blackie did look like a show dog.

"And he can do tricks. Let's show him, Blackie."

Danny scrambled out of the armchair and pulled a Frisbee from under the dining-room table. He threw it toward Jerry. Blackie lunged and intercepted it, then dropped it at Jerry's feet.

"He wants you to throw it," Danny said. Jerry's throw went high, straight for a shelf of figurines. Blackie leaped three feet off the ground and caught it.

"Good dog!" Jerry patted him on the head.

They began to fling the Frisbee back and forth. Blackie's antics were amazing. Danny's face was red from laughing. For the first time since Jerry had met him, he looked happy, not like in class when he'd made some funny remark and gotten everyone's attention, but really happy.

The front door opened.

"Danny! Not in the house!" A woman with curly blond hair began swinging grocery bags from the porch into the living room.

"Mom, did you see how high Blackie jumped?"

"He's ready for the Olympics, but I'd like my lamps in one piece, thanks." She saw Jerry. "Hi. I'm Danny's mother."

"This is Jerry Wheelock, Mom. He's a friend from school."

"It's nice to meet you, Mrs. Casey," Jerry said. Feeling guilty, he grabbed two of the bags and carried them into the kitchen.

"Hey, thanks," Danny's mother said. "You can come by anytime."

Danny brought the rest of the bags into the kitchen. His mother began putting the groceries away.

"Learn anything at school? Or was it a regular day?"

"Regular."

"Did you bring in the mail?"

Danny went to the porch and came back with a stack of envelopes. His mother glanced at each one and tossed it on the table. Most of them were addressed to "Kathleen Casey."

"Junk, junk, bill, more junk. Here's the support check from your father. I guess it got stuck in the mail."

That explained about Danny's father.

"What's for dinner?" said Danny.

"Warthog on toast."

"Whole wheat or white?" Danny shot back.

"Whole wheat. We're out of white." She opened the refrigerator. "Oh, too bad. We finished the warthog last night. I guess we'll have to have chicken."

Jerry began to see where Danny got his talent for wisecracks.

Danny's mother dumped a bag of corn chips into a bowl. Danny opened a jar of salsa and a package of cheese. Jerry wasn't supposed to snack before dinner, but a couple of chips wouldn't count. Maybe a small handful. Or two. By the time he looked at the clock and saw that it was eight minutes after six, he wasn't very hungry anymore.

Sherlock

The next morning, Jerry had an idea as he was getting ready for school. What if he could track down Jennifer Atwood and interview her? The trouble was, as far as he knew the Atwoods no longer lived in town. He asked his mother about them at breakfast.

"They moved a few months after it happened," she said. "Jennifer Atwood might be married now and have a different last name. I don't know how you'd find her. All I remember is that her father's first name was Quentin. Why don't you just interview Charles?"

"I will, but Mrs. Finneran said to use more than one source if we could." Jerry thought how amazed

Charles would be if he could tell him what happened to Jennifer after all these years.

After the lunch bell that day, Jerry stayed behind to double-check the reading assignment with Pamela. Danny was waiting for him at the door to the cafeteria. Jerry hadn't been expecting that.

"Come on, Jer. I saw a couple of places we can sit together."

This time, Danny rummaged around and found Ginger Chicken sandwiches.

"Well," said Danny, after he took a bite, "you can't win 'em all. I once ate a caterpillar."

"Did somebody dare you?"

"No. I just wanted to see what it tasted like."

"And?"

"I was surprised. It was really good. Kind of squishy, though."

"You're kidding."

Danny burst out laughing. "Of course I'm kidding. It was horrible."

Jerry told Danny about his idea to find the person Charles had rescued.

"That would be great, Jerry. How are you going to do it?"

"I don't know yet. I just thought of it this morning."

After lunch, Jerry was on his way to his locker when he ran into Phil.

"Jerry, are you ever going to eat lunch with us again?"

"It's only until Danny makes some friends here."

"At the rate he's going, my guess is that you're it."

Jerry knew he had a problem, but for the rest of the week he was able to dodge it. Danny's special program kept him busy after school. During the lunch period on Thursday, Jerry had to return some library books. He got to the cafeteria late, and Danny had already left. On Friday, Danny got sent to Mr. Harrison's office again. By the time he got to lunch, Jerry—sitting with his friends—was almost finished.

That night, Jerry decided to call his seventeen-year-old cousin Nate Farnsworth to ask for help with his plan to find Jennifer Atwood. Nate always had good ideas.

"Sure," he said when Jerry phoned him. "Stop by tomorrow."

When Jerry got to the Farnsworths' house the

next morning, his cousin was in his room, examining the telescope kit he had ordered.

"Jerry, check out my new toy."

Given Nate's thick glasses and the white shirts he always wore, Jerry realized that his cousin looked like a classic nerd. But Nate was so unruffled by the possibility, and so brainy, that a lot of people, like Jerry, thought he was cool.

"Of course, I'll have to grind the lens for this baby. That's the key to the whole thing."

He handed Jerry a pad of paper and a pencil. "So you're trying to locate the Atwoods. What's the most obvious place to look for someone's address? Normally, I mean."

"The phone book."

"Right. Of course we have a slight complication in this case."

"We don't know which phone book to look in."

"Right again. How many phone books do you suppose there are in the United States?"

"Hundreds?"

"Probably thousands. So looking book by book would be a bit labor-intensive. But—"

"But?"

"If you had a magic wand, what would you do? Assuming you couldn't use it to point to the right book."

Jerry thought. "Use it to mash all the phone books together into one big book?"

"Fortunately, somebody's already done that. All the phone listings in the country are combined on a set of CD-ROMs. The library has them. Have the librarian show you how to use them."

"That's great!" Jerry wrote "CD-ROM phone book" on his pad.

"But—"

"The Atwoods might have an unlisted number."

"Right. Now let's imagine," said Nate, "that your long-lost buddy Fred comes through town. He wants to look up his old pal Jerry Wheelock. He's forgotten your address and you're not listed in the phone book. What could he do?"

"He could ask somebody at a store or a lunch place or something like that. Maybe he'd find somebody who knows me. I already thought of trying to find old friends of the Atwoods," Jerry said, writing it on his pad.

"Or relatives."

Jerry added "family" to his list.

"How do I find friends or relatives?"

"Who are the first people you usually make friends with when you move to a new place?"

"The neighbors. I'll go talk to the neighbors."

"And the relatives?"

"The phone book," said Jerry.

"You catch on quick. But we need a few more ideas."

"I could talk to the people who own their house now. Maybe they know where the Atwoods went."

"You're a regular bloodhound. You just gave me an idea. When a house is sold, who usually handles the sale?"

"A real estate agent. Maybe I can find the agent."

"And the Atwoods might have had a lawyer besides the agent."

Jerry looked at his list. He had six ideas.

"Thanks, Nate. One of these has got to work."

"Two great deductive minds are better than one," said his cousin, opening the directions for his telescope kit. "Let me know how you make out, Sherlock."

By the following Saturday, Jerry hadn't made out too well.

Not one Quentin Atwood was listed on the CD-ROMs.

The Atwoods' old house turned out to be one of five on a dead-end street, Elmgrove Terrace. Two of the families had moved in after the Atwoods left. The elderly woman who lived across the street had known them only slightly. The next-door neighbors were away on a trip.

The elderly neighbor did remember that the Atwoods had been friends with the people who owned the gift shop on Sayer Street. The friends said they had exchanged a few letters with the Atwoods after they moved. Then the Atwoods moved again and the correspondence stopped.

No other Atwoods were listed in the local phone book.

The owners of the Atwoods' old house had bought it only three years ago.

Jerry found the real estate agent by phoning the agencies in town, one after another. The agent remembered the Atwoods but had no information, although she did know the lawyer who had advised them.

The lawyer had died.

Jerry had one hope left. The elderly neighbor had told him that the next-door neighbors would be back the following Saturday, June 12. That morning, Jerry was on his way out the door to talk to them when the phone rang. His father answered.

"It's Danny," he said, handing Jerry the phone.

Jerry hadn't seen Danny outside of class the previous week. After his last trip to Mr. Harrison's office, Danny had been assigned to an additional social skills class that met during the lunch period. He ate in the Special Programs room with the other students in the group. Jerry had found that lunch wasn't as interesting without him.

"Hello?"

"Hi, Jer. I'm going to KaZam. How long will it take you to get there?"

"I've got an errand to run," said Jerry. "Maybe we can get together later."

"Where's your errand?"

"I don't think you know the place. It's Elmgrove Terrace."

"I know it. Are you leaving now?"

"Well—"

"I'll meet you there."

Danny wasn't easily discouraged.

When Jerry got to number 27, he rang the door-bell, but nobody answered. He felt his last chance slipping away.

"Hey, Jerry!" Danny waved from down the street. "All done?"

Jerry walked back down the sidewalk. "They're not home."

"Who?"

"The people who live in this house might know the family I'm trying to find for my report."

"Is this where they used to live?"

"The gray house." Jerry pointed. "I'm pretty much out of ideas."

"Oh, you can come back tomorrow." Danny made a dismissive gesture. "Come with me. We can go to a great place in the woods for animal watching. It's right near here."

Jerry didn't want to go to the woods. He wanted to talk with Nate. But Nate was away this weekend on a family trip.

"Okay."

Danny broke into a smile. "I know a shortcut. Fol-low me."

"Did you get an idea for your report yet?" Jerry said as they walked to the end of the street.

"Yeah. From Mrs. Finneran. She told me that the library used to be a train station. Mrs. Tracy in the reference room showed me how to find the blueprints of the old station. They're pretty interesting. You can see a lot of stuff is still there—like the ticket booth. That's where they keep the videos now."

When they reached the fence that divided the woods from the last house lot, Danny showed Jerry an opening to slip through.

In a few hundred yards, they intersected the main trail and followed it to a sign with arrows for Miller's Creek Bridge and Eagle Bluff. They started toward the bridge. Before they reached it, Danny veered off the trail. A short uphill climb brought them to a clearing.

"See that?"

At first, Jerry couldn't make out what Danny was pointing to.

"I think it's an old hunting blind. I don't think anybody uses it now."

At the edge of the clearing, Jerry made out a

crude shelter, almost completely camouflaged by leaves and branches.

"My luxury condo," said Danny, crawling into the blind. Jerry backed in and sat down on the carpet of dried leaves.

"Of course, there's a lot of chipmunks and squirrels, but I saw a hawk here once," Danny said, "and last week I saw a woodchuck. You have to be real quiet."

That sounded funny coming from Danny.

Jerry eased himself farther into the blind. Leaves crackled under him.

"Try not to move," said Danny.

Jerry settled into what seemed like a good position, but after a few minutes he began to feel like he was sitting on concrete. Bees droned. A chickadee called. Not a single animal appeared.

He could be seeing if the Atwoods' old neighbors had come home. He could be riding his bike. He could be—

Danny squeezed Jerry's arm and pointed.

About thirty feet from the blind, a doe had stepped out of the wall of greenery. Her ears twitched and her nostrils flared as she scanned her surroundings. Then she began feeding on a low bush at the edge of the clearing. Every few seconds, she raised her head to look around.

Reaching for more leaves, she took another step, then another and another, each time closer to the blind. Jerry hardly dared to breathe.

He'd been close to deer before, the ones in the enclosure at the zoo. He'd even fed them through the chain-link fence. They seemed to be delicate creatures, with their dreamy eyes and stick legs. Now, hunched on the ground with only a flimsy barrier for protection, he sensed the power in the lean, muscular body and the legs that tapered to sharp hooves. This was a wild animal, alert and unpredictable.

Jerry never saw what it was—maybe a squirrel's discarded acorn cap—but something fell out of one of the trees. It hit the ground with a dull thud. The doe whirled around. In a blur of motion, she crashed back into the tall shrubs and disappeared.

He and Danny looked at each other. Neither of them spoke.

"I never saw a deer before," Danny said at last. "I didn't think they came out in the daytime."

"Me either."

"The wind must have been blowing our scent the other way."

"Do you think we'll see another one?"

"Not today," said Danny. "If any others were around, they'd have been spooked by all the noise."

Jerry stood up and shook his foot. "Pins and needles," he said. "Hey, Danny, we're not too far from the plaque I told you about, the one that tells about my cousin saving the little girl. Want to see it?"

"Sure."

They went to the trail and backtracked to the sign for Eagle Bluff. When they reached the top, Jerry found the plaque almost covered with vines. Remembering that Danny had a problem, Jerry read the inscription out loud. It told the story, in brief, that he had found at the library.

"So he was eighteen," Danny said. "My uncle was about that old when he stole his first car, just for a joyride."

"He was in high school?"

"No, he'd already dropped out by then."

"Did he live around here?"

"Yeah, he grew up in the house I live in. I've

got his old room. Want to look at the ledge?"

"Okay." Jerry did not want to look at the ledge. Heights made him dizzy. "When you get close to the drop-off, go on your stomach. It's safer."

Danny didn't seem to be concerned about safety, but he did get on all fours to peer down. Jerry crawled up beside him.

"That's not much of a ledge," said Danny.

"It's pretty narrow," said Jerry, trying to stay focused on near objects. The scene below seemed to tilt crazily. What would hanging in space by a thin rope be like?

"I'll bet rock climbing would be fun," said Danny.

Jerry backed away from the edge and stood up. "The people I came to see might be home now. It's after one o'clock."

"It is?" said Danny. "I've got to get home. My mom had to work today. I'm supposed to walk Blackie."

They split up at the opening in the fence that bordered the woods. Jerry returned to the house on Elmgrove Terrace. This time the neighbors were home. Yes, they remembered the Atwoods well. No, they didn't know where the family had gone.

His great idea had fizzled. Or had it? He'd focused on one feature story. What if the *Courier* had run other stories, maybe one on the Atwoods? He checked his watch. One-thirty. The library closed at two on Saturday. He started to run.

"You'll have to find what you need quickly," said Mrs. Tracy as Jerry sat down at a microfilm reader. She handed him a box.

"Thanks, Mrs. Tracy."

With his pulse still pounding from the run, he loaded the film and raced his time machine to July 26. He scanned every page. Nothing. But on the front page for July 27, a headline caught his eye: "Atwoods Express Gratitude to Daughter's Rescuer." The photo showed a dark-haired woman handing a book to Charles. Jerry read the caption.

"From her collection of rare books, Jennifer's mother Ruth gives Charles Findlay an edition of *Scaling the Heights*, a classic work on climbing, long out of print."

A store in town sold rare books. Maybe Jennifer's mother used to buy things there.

"Jerry, the library's closing in five minutes," said Mrs. Tracy from the doorway.

"That's okay. I think I found what I need."

He rushed to the Avid Reader. Closed. Jerry read the sign: "On vacation May 29–June 13. See you on Monday, June 14—Alice Hammond."

On Monday, Jerry went straight to the bookstore after school. He introduced himself to the woman who ran it and explained why he wanted to find the Atwoods.

"Well," she said, "I don't give out the phone numbers and addresses of people on my mailing list, but I can make a call for you." She opened a small box of index cards and flipped through it. "Here we are." She dialed the number. "Hello, Ruth? This is Alice Hammond."

After she explained the situation, the person on the other end of the line spoke for several minutes. Mrs. Hammond kept nodding. "Yes . . . yes . . . I understand . . . of course. Just a minute, I'll tell him."

She looked up at Jerry. "Mrs. Atwood will pass along your phone number to her daughter and give her your message."

Mrs. Hammond repeated the number Jerry gave her.

"Thank you, Ruth . . . Yes, you too. Goodbye."

She hung up the phone. "Now, she's not saying that her daughter will definitely call you."

"I understand. Thanks, Mrs. Hammond. I really mean it. This was my last chance."

Jerry hurried home. That evening at eight-thirty, the phone rang. He raced to answer. "Hello, the Wheelocks'."

"Hi, this is Jennifer Martin. May I speak to Jerry?"

"This is Jerry."

"I got your message. I'd be happy to talk with you. I live in Westerfield. Can you get here? Or should we do this on the phone?"

Westerfield was only eighty miles away, and Jerry did not like talking on the phone. A four-way conversation with his parents on the extension, plus one call to the Farnsworths, settled the matter. On the following Saturday, Jerry would take the bus to Westerfield with his cousin Nate.

Saturday was June 19. Jerry was cutting it close for a June 22 deadline. But for Jennifer's first-person story the risk was worth it.

Jerry decided not to say anything to his friends, including Danny, about finding Jennifer. He also asked his parents not to give away the secret. He wanted to surprise everyone with the story.

At school, Danny was the only one who knew he was even looking for her. Jerry didn't know what he'd say if Danny asked him how the search was going.

But Danny didn't ask. Jerry realized that the search—which was constantly on his mind—wasn't on Danny's radar screen. Sometimes Jerry wondered if Danny had a radar screen. He never seemed to notice when Jerry, or anybody else, was irritated with him or when he'd pushed a joke too far. Jerry couldn't make sense of it. Danny wasn't stupid.

On Wednesday, Phil started telling Jerry that he was worried because his pet white rat had started pulling out some of his fur. Danny overheard the conversation and cut Phil short. "He's bored. Put lots of toys in the cage, different ones every day."

"Mind your own business," said Phil, but on Friday he told Jerry that he'd tried it and it worked.

If Danny could figure that out, why couldn't he tell how other people felt? It was a mystery.

Tiger by the Tail

The next Saturday, Jerry and Nate boarded the noon bus to Westerfield. During the hour-and-a-half ride, Jerry went over his list of questions with his cousin Nate. The list wasn't long. What he needed from Jennifer wasn't information about what happened. He already had that. He wanted her to describe how she had felt.

Following Jennifer's directions from the station, Jerry and Nate walked the dozen blocks to her home. When Jerry rang the bell, a plump woman with red hair and a baby on her hip came to the door. Jerry was about to ask for Jennifer Martin when he realized this was Jennifer. He'd been picturing her as a skinny five-year-old.

"Hi, you're Jerry? And you're Nate." She smiled and pushed open the screen door. "Come on in. Excuse the mess." The living room was littered with baby toys, blankets, and a playpen. "Why don't you take the sofa?" She sat down in an armchair and reached for a baby bottle.

"Where should we start?"

Jerry opened his notepad. He was nervous at first, but when Jennifer began to tell her story he forgot about his discomfort.

She described how she'd thought she could get to her grandmother's house by going through the woods.

"Kids are so silly. I must have gotten the notion from 'over the river and through the woods, to Grandmother's house we go.' My grandmother lived about fifty miles away.

"I got onto this path somehow. It went up and up. I thought sure it would take me to the house, but I wound up on top of a cliff. I looked over the edge and saw a river."

"Miller's Creek," Jerry said.

"Is that what it's called? I think I must have been crying and not seeing where I was going. All of a sudden, I fell. I think I slid part of the way. Then I hit the ledge."

"Did it hurt a lot?"

"I guess it must have, but I don't remember about that. I remember tucking my knees under my skirt and sitting there waiting for my parents to come get me."

She lifted the baby to her shoulder.

"I waited and waited. I couldn't understand why nobody came. I got cold, and I was so frightened, especially when it started to rain. I curled up and tried to go to sleep."

"And then Charles came."

"Yes. I had been crying again, I think, because I didn't hear him until he was right beside me. He said he was going to take me home and that my mom and dad would be so happy to see me.

"He said that I was being very brave and that he needed my help. He made a kind of harness out of rope. I had to get into it. Then he told me to close my eyes. He tied me to him somehow, but my legs were dangling."

Jerry's stomach turned over at the thought. "That must have been awful."

"It was. I remember clutching his shirt. But he kept talking to me, telling me how much my parents loved me and that I'd be seeing them soon. And then we were at the top. One of the other men put his jacket on me."

"That must have been later," Jerry said. "Charles didn't meet up with the other searchers for about twenty minutes. That's what the paper said."

Jennifer looked confused. "Oh, I thought someone was right there. Maybe I got mixed up. Anyway, I remember Charles very well. When we got to the top, he set me on my feet and I opened my eyes. He was wearing a blue shirt with the sleeves rolled up. I especially remember the tattoo on his arm."

"Tattoo?" Jerry thought he hadn't heard right.

"Yes, I'd never seen one before and I thought it was very strange."

"What kind of tattoo was it?"

"It was a wildcat of some kind."

"A cougar?"

"Yes, that was it. Did he have it removed? Lots of people do."

"Uh, I guess he did." Jerry could hardly think of

what he was saying. Jennifer's memory had to be wrong. If she'd said anything about a tattoo, sooner or later everyone would have known about it.

"You told the reporters from the *Courier* about all this? About the tattoo and everything?"

"Oh, no, my parents kept reporters away from me. I think that the newspaper wanted me to pose for a photo with Charles, but my parents wouldn't allow it. They were afraid that answering a lot of questions would cause me to relive the incident. I'm sure that's why we moved a few months later. As it was, I couldn't talk about what happened for a long time afterward—years."

Jerry was grateful that his cousin was there. For the next few minutes, Nate kept the conversation going while Jerry scribbled notes in his pad to hide his confusion.

Then Jennifer had to put the baby down for a nap. Jerry and Nate got up to go.

"Thanks a million for talking to us," Jerry said.

"I was happy to do it." Jennifer opened the screen door for them. "Your cousin saved my life and I'll never forget him."

Nate put out his hand. "A pleasure meeting you."

"And you." She shook his hand, then Jerry's. "Good luck with that report!"

On the way to the station, Jerry told Nate about Danny's uncle and the tattoo he had.

"Well," Nate said, "it looks like you've got a tiger by the tail now. Or shall I say a cougar?"

"Ha-ha."

"It is a puzzle. Do you suppose Charles had a tattoo and got rid of it?"

They looked at each other and shook their heads.

"You know," said Nate, "about twenty people saw him carrying Jennifer across the field to Chandler's Lodge."

"She said that another man was there at the top of Eagle Bluff."

"I know. Of course, she could be mistaken," said Nate. "It was a long time ago, and she must have been pretty upset."

"Right." Jerry began to feel better. He'd been sickened at first to think that Charles hadn't told the truth about what happened.

But she was so definite about the tattoo.

As the bus pulled onto the main highway, Jerry kept turning the problem over in his mind.

"Penny for your thoughts," said Nate.

"I don't have to tell Charles—or anybody else—about the tattoo. And when I write my report, I could just leave it out."

"You could. What would happen then?"

"Nothing. Everybody would be happy."

"Including you?"

Jerry looked at Nate. "No," he said at last. "I guess I wouldn't be."

"I didn't think so," said Nate. "That wouldn't be like you." They rode in silence for another minute. "Are you going to ask Charles about Jennifer's story?"

"I think I've got to."

Jerry didn't want any shadows on his friendship with Charles. In his heart, he felt that Charles would have an explanation, something that would clear up the confusion and put everything back in place again.

But Jerry could hardly picture asking him the question. And the whole problem was his own stupid fault for being so stubborn about finding Jennifer.

The bus arrived back in town on schedule. As the driver stopped for a light at Sayer Street, Jerry noticed a squad car in front of McGrath's Comics. Then he saw Danny being escorted into the back seat by Lieutenant Hanlon.

"Could you let me off here?" Jerry called to the driver. "Nate, I've got to go. That's Danny over there."

"Let me know what you find out."

Lieutenant Hanlon had started the car by the time Jerry got across the street. He ran to the passenger-side window.

"Could I go with you? Danny's a friend of mine."

"It's Jerry Wheelock, isn't it?"

"Yes, you know my dad."

"Okay, Jerry, get in the front seat. I'm afraid your friend was caught shoplifting. Mr. McGrath's tired of people stealing merchandise. He decided to take some action and I don't blame him."

Jerry didn't know what to say. They drove to the station house in silence.

When they got there, Lieutenant Hanlon told them to sit in the chairs by his desk.

"I'll be right back." He went to another office.

"Did you really take something?" Jerry whispered.

Danny shrugged. "A couple of comic books. You'd think he could spare a few."

"Didn't you have the money?"

"I sort of did. But I guess I've got those Maguire larceny genes." He gave his wise-guy grin.

At that moment, Jerry would have given anything to be able to tell Danny that the Maguires had more than that. They had courage, too. But he couldn't say anything, not before he'd talked to Charles. And what he'd heard from Jennifer was probably a simple mix-up anyway.

Lieutenant Hanlon came back with a handful of forms.

"You know, Danny," he said, "this is how your uncle started out. I'd hate to see you going the same way."

Danny leaned back in his chair in an attitude of cool defiance. "Well, us Maguires have a talent, you know what I mean?"

"And that's the kind of attitude that will wreck

your life, you know what I mean?" He watched Danny for a minute. Then he said, "How old were you the last time you saw your uncle?"

"Four. When they let him out for my grandma's funeral."

"I'd forgotten about that. What do you remember about him?"

"Everything."

"Did you see much of him? Before his second prison term, I mean. He didn't live here."

"He liked to move around. But he used to come over to our place a lot."

"Danny, I was the officer who arrested your uncle for joyriding in a stolen car when he was seventeen. It was one of my first collars as a rookie."

Danny smiled. "But he gave you the slip, didn't he?"

"Yes, and it's too bad, because all those years after he jumped bail on the joyriding charge, your mother and her folks had no idea where he was. Eight years later, our department was notified about his arrest for auto theft because we had an outstanding warrant for him. That night, I went to your house to tell the Maguires. Your mother cried. She was a sophomore in high school and her brother—who could have been dead for all she knew—was about to go to prison."

Danny sat forward in his chair, almost spitting out the words. "How my mother feels isn't any of your business, is it?"

"No, Danny, it's yours. I phoned her when we got to the station and told her I'd drop you off home. She's pretty upset."

Danny slumped in his chair and turned away.

"Jerry," Lieutenant Hanlon continued, "I called your father, too. He's coming by to pick you up. You can wait here. Danny, let's go."

Danny turned around at the door. "Bye, Jer. If they send me to the Big House, you can bake me a cake with a file in it."

Another time, that would have been funny.

Jerry's father arrived a few minutes later. As they got into the car, he said, "Sounds like you've had an interesting day."

It had been more interesting than his father knew.

They pulled out onto Bridgewater Avenue.

"Jerry, I know a little about Danny since the

school board arranged for his transfer. I realize he's had a hard time. I suppose you know at least some of the reasons why. But I'm concerned about you. I see that Danny is looking for your friendship, but I'm afraid he's trouble. I won't forbid you to see him, but I want you to think about what I've said."

Jerry had been thinking about his friendship with Danny, about Danny's demands on his attention, the tug-of-war between him and Jerry's other friends. For all the problems, Jerry didn't want to give up the friendship. He really liked Danny. But he didn't know how to fix what was wrong.

Nobody said much of anything at dinner that night. When it was over, Jerry carried the dishes to his mother at the sink.

"Mom, did Charles Findlay ever get a tattoo? I mean when he was in high school? That he had removed?"

His mother looked surprised, then amused.

"Charles? He didn't even wear sneakers to school. He wore leather shoes. No tattoos, I guarantee you."

Jerry lay awake a long time that night, his mind

full of warring thoughts. Jennifer had to be mistaken. That was the explanation. A simple question to Charles would settle that. In fact, Jerry didn't need to ask him.

But the tiny doubt wouldn't stay quiet. If Jennifer wasn't mistaken, would Charles have an explanation? Was Jerry being fair if he didn't ask him what it was? And what was fair to Jack Maguire? If the truth came out, would it help Danny's uncle? What was the truth?

Charles knew. The next morning, Jerry called him. He explained that he was doing a report for social studies that would be read on Awards Night at his school.

"I want to interview you about something that happened a long time ago," Jerry began. He cleared his throat nervously.

Charles broke in. "I'll do my best to help, Jerry. You know, being on a battlefield isn't the way you see it in the movies. A lot of the time, you're so scared and miserable, you hardly know what you're doing."

Jerry was caught off guard. He was so focused on the rescue that he hadn't realized that Charles would assume the topic was his war experiences. Jerry knew he should set Charles straight on the real reason for the interview, but he couldn't find the words fast enough.

"Why don't you stop by my office tomorrow after school?" Charles said.

Jerry would have to find the words by then.

"Okay. See you."

The Interview

Charles worked in the center of town, in a stone building facing Washington Park. As Jerry went up the marble steps on Monday afternoon, he remembered having been inside once before, when his father needed to check a survey map.

Charles's office had a view of the park through an arched window. When Jerry presented himself at the door, Charles was on the phone.

"Bill, I've got to go. We'll talk tomorrow." He hung up. "Jerry! It's so nice to see someone who isn't wearing a pencil protector in his pocket. Come on in." He scooped a stack of papers off a leather chair. "Here. Take the good chair. I save the uncomfortable chair for people I don't want to talk to."

Jerry sat down.

"So tell me about this report."

Jerry took a deep breath. "On the phone you thought it was about what you did in Vietnam. I should have told you—it isn't. My report is going to be about the time you rescued the little girl from the ledge."

"Oh." For several seconds, Charles looked at Jerry without saying anything. When he spoke, his voice was quieter than before. "I see. I haven't talked about that for a long time. Not since it happened, really. I guess you've heard stories about it from the family."

Jerry nodded.

"You know," Charles said, "these things get exaggerated over time."

Jerry had brought his copy of the article from the *Courier*. He pulled it out of his pocket and handed it to his cousin.

Charles skimmed the photocopy. "I don't believe I ever read this. It certainly makes me out to be a hero, doesn't it?" He swiveled his chair around and looked out the window. Jerry sensed the opening he was looking for.

"You don't think you were?"

"In a tough spot, people just do what they have to," said Charles. "Hero is a label other people put on you afterward."

"I have a question to ask you." Jerry heard his voice going hoarse. "Did the newspaper get everything right? Is this the way it happened?"

Charles continued looking out the window for what seemed like a long time. Then he turned around and faced Jerry.

"No, Jerry, this isn't the way it happened. I was there, but I wasn't alone. Somebody else was the real hero."

"Somebody who had a cougar tattoo?"

"Yes. How did you know that?"

"Jennifer Atwood told me. I found her. She's Jennifer Martin now. I talked to her on Saturday. Jennifer thinks you're the one who got her off the ledge. But she remembers that the person who did had a cougar tattoo."

"He did." In the silence that followed, Jerry could feel his pulse pounding in his ears.

"I must look like a fraud to you now," said Charles.

"I figured you'd be able to explain everything."

"I can explain, Jerry, but I haven't got any excuses."

"Who was with you?"

"His name was Jack Maguire. I'd met him when I was rock climbing. He was a year younger than I was, but he'd been climbing a lot longer. He gave me some pointers. We started climbing together."

"You got to be friends?"

"We got to be climbing buddies. That's different. Climbing was the only thing we had in common. Jack was in with a bad crowd. He was always in trouble with the police, mostly minor stuff. So we didn't pal around. But out on the bluffs, I saw a different side of him. When you're climbing, you have to be able to trust your partner—trust him with your life. I always knew I could trust Jack.

"The odd thing is," Charles said, handing the photocopy back, "except for a couple of minor things about handling the rope, everything in this article is true—only it combines my experience and Jack's. That's the part I've never told anybody. While I was hiking to the top of Eagle Bluff, I met Jack."

"He was out climbing? Wasn't it kind of late?"

"He was on the run. He told me he'd been arrested for stealing a car to go joyriding. His folks had made bail. He was due in court in two days, but he was going to skip."

"Wouldn't everybody know by morning that he was gone?"

"He was hardly living at home. Friends often put him up, so even his parents wouldn't know until his court date that he was missing. I tried to talk him into going back, but he wouldn't listen. He made out that he was this tough guy, but I think he was scared."

Jerry thought of Danny at the police station.

Charles took a sip of his coffee and continued. "He planned to hike over the top of Eagle Bluff and down to the highway. He figured he could hitch a ride from there. I was still trying to talk him out of running when we got to the top and heard Jennifer. We looked over the edge and saw her dislodge that loose rock. I said I'd get her. Jack convinced me not to. He said that if I couldn't make it I'd kill myself and her. He was the better climber. He went down."

Charles set the coffee cup back on the desk. "I

did do one thing. While Jack rappelled to the ledge, I took a second rope and anchored myself to the tree. Then I sat near the edge with my feet braced and my hands on Jack's rope. When he was able to, Jack tied one end of his rope to his harness and let go of the other end. I pulled that free end up and passed it around me. As he moved up the cliff, I kept shuffling the rope through my hands, taking up the slack. If Jack had slipped, I would have caught him before he fell more than an inch or two. But he didn't slip."

"You didn't use the rope to pull him up?"

"Only at the end, the last few feet. He looked like he was having trouble."

"Maybe he was. Maybe he wouldn't have made it without your help."

"No. Jack was tired, but he would have made it."

They sat in silence for a moment. Jerry struggled to sort out the tangle of what-ifs. He was sure that Charles was selling himself short.

"Wait. Bringing the climbing gear was your idea. How could Jack have rescued anybody without that?"

"You have to understand," said Charles, "the rope

was only for insurance. Jack was skilled enough—
and strong enough—to climb without it."

"What about carrying Jennifer?"

At first, Jerry was sure that he'd hit on something
solid that Charles couldn't dismiss. His cousin
thought for several seconds before he answered.

"He could have used his belt or his shirt to tie her
to him. Jack was a resourceful guy."

Jerry couldn't think of another way to counter
Charles's refusal to take any credit. He had to go
on.

"And when they got to the top, you put your
jacket on Jennifer."

"Does she remember that?"

"Yes. She remembers that another man was
there."

"After what he'd done, I was sure that Jack
wouldn't be sent to jail, but he wouldn't change his
mind. He begged me not to tell anybody that I'd
seen him, to say that I'd rescued Jennifer—at least
until the police found out that he'd gone."

"You could have told the truth when they did find
out."

"I could have. But I didn't. I kept thinking I

would, but everything happened so fast. Jerry, you don't know what it is to have people suddenly honoring you as a hero. Sometimes it's not wonderful. It's like being cornered. You think of all the people who believe in you who'll be let down. My father had died the year before, and my mother still hadn't recovered. This meant everything to her."

He took another sip of his coffee.

"I couldn't take it. I was supposed to go away to college that fall, but I couldn't wait that long to get away. I enlisted in the Army. Since I wasn't sure how I felt about the war, I asked to be trained as a medic."

"So you ran away, like Jack did."

"Yes, I ran away."

"And you got sent to Vietnam."

Charles nodded. "As soon as my training was over. At least it was a chance to earn my reputation as a hero."

"How long were you there?"

"A year. Then I served three more in the States."

"What about when you got back? Couldn't you have told everybody then? You had the medals. Nobody would have minded."

"Jerry, I know it's hard to understand this, but when I got home my whole life before Vietnam seemed a million miles away. Jack had disappeared. I packed my bags for college and never looked back."

"Jack is in prison."

"Is he? How do you know that?"

"Danny told me."

"Danny?"

"Danny Casey. You met him at my house. Jack's his uncle, his mother's brother. Her name is Kathleen."

Charles sat back in his chair, a look of wonder on his face. "Jack told me he had a little sister named Kathleen. She couldn't have been much older than Jennifer. So Danny is her son. What's he like?"

"He likes to wisecrack a lot and sometimes he's really funny, but he gets in trouble for it. He's different from other people. He knows about things that other people don't."

"What does he think about his uncle?"

"He wants to be just like him."

"Oh, no. That mustn't be allowed to happen." Charles thought for a minute. "Write the story,

Jerry. Write exactly what I've told you. But please don't say anything to anybody until the awards ceremony. I don't want half-truths getting around. I'd like to make a statement afterward. I'll call Mrs. Finneran. I think I can arrange it."

"Nate was with me when I talked to Jennifer Martin. Can I tell him?"

"Sure. Nate will keep it to himself."

Jerry said goodbye. As he walked down the corridor, he picked up speed. By the time he flagged the bus on Bridgewater, he was in a dead run. The report was due in the morning.

When Jerry got home, he went straight to his room. Dinner was a sandwich eaten at his desk. At eleven o'clock, he stacked the pages of his report, turned out the light, and crawled into bed still dressed. He thought he should get up and put on his pajamas. Then he fell asleep.

Jerry steered clear of the cafeteria on Tuesday afternoon, spending the lunch period in the library. He felt like a criminal hiding out, but he didn't want to be drawn into any conversations about his report. Nate was the only person besides Charles who knew what was in it. Jerry had managed to make a quiet phone call to him the previous evening.

Danny stopped him on the way back to class.

"Where were you?"

"The library. I didn't feel like having lunch." That was true as far as it went.

"Are you sick or something?"

"No, I'm sort of beat, though. I was up late last night."

"Me too. I had most of that report to do. I would have bet you had yours done days ago. By the way, did you ever track down the person you were looking for?"

Just then, Phil ran up to them. "Hey, there's a bird flying around the cafeteria."

"How did it get in?" said Jerry.

"Who knows, but Mr. Harrison and Mrs. Arnold are trying to catch it. You don't want to miss the show."

They ran down the stairs in time to see the confused bird light on the cash register. Mr. Harrison dropped a brown paper bag over it, then headed for the back door to release it.

To Jerry's relief, Danny's question was forgotten.

Wednesday was the first of three half-days at school. That morning, Danny launched into a tale of woe about having to spend what otherwise would have been free afternoons doing chores at McGrath's to make up for the comic books he'd stolen.

Just then, Jerry didn't want the situation turned into material for one of Danny's funny monologues. He said the first thing that came to him.

"Was your mother angry when you got home from the police station?"

Danny's bravado evaporated. "Yeah, for a while. Then she said I'd let her down. She never said that before."

He showed Jerry the letter of apology he and his mother had agreed he should write to Mr. McGrath. She had helped him with it, since he had a hard time putting things on paper, but he was supposed to repeat the apology in person that afternoon. He was not looking forward to the experience.

"But I promised her I'd never let her down again," he said.

On Thursday morning, Jerry was opening his locker when he heard Danny's voice behind him.

"After you're done sweeping a sidewalk, do you know how long it takes for more garbage to blow in? About two seconds flat."

Jerry turned around. "Did you read your letter to Mr. McGrath?"

Danny nodded. "It wasn't as hard as I thought. After I was through, Mr. McGrath told me that shoplifting costs him more money every year than he makes in a whole week. I never realized he lost that much. I figured it was just a couple of bucks here and there."

Jerry had a feeling that shoplifting would not be a problem for Danny anymore.

Lucky Man

At the awards ceremony on Friday evening, Jerry sat on the stage waiting nervously. His report was scheduled last. That must mean that Charles had talked to Mrs. Finneran.

One by one, students had read, then taken seats in the auditorium. Now only Jerry and Danny were left as Pamela Woodward exited the stage to a round of applause. Danny got up, carrying two drawings on poster board. Instead of reading, he held up the drawings, copied from blueprints, and talked about how the old train station had been reconstructed into the present-day library.

From the whispers among his classmates, Jerry knew they were surprised that Danny could do so well. When the applause came at the end, Danny leaned close to the microphone.

"Thanks. You've been a great audience." It was a perfect imitation of comics Jerry had seen on TV. Laughter rippled through the auditorium.

Mrs. Finneran gave Danny a quick victory sign as she stepped up to the microphone. "We have one last report before we conclude our program this evening. It was prepared by Jeremiah Wheelock. As many of you know, Jerry is a cousin of Charles Findlay, head of our town planning board, who was awarded the Silver Star, as well as a Purple Heart, for his bravery as a medic during the Vietnam conflict. The report concerns Mr. Findlay, who has asked to say a few words after Jerry has concluded."

She nodded to Charles, who stood at the side of the stage.

A buzz went around the auditorium. Jerry came forward and began to read.

"On an evening in July, almost thirty years ago, a daring rescue was performed on Eagle Bluff. The life of a little girl was saved.

"The adventure began when Jennifer Atwood, who was only five years old, thought she could get to her grandmother's house by going through the woods. She was thinking of the song 'over the river and through the woods . . .' "

As Jerry read the opening paragraphs, the buzz of voices died down to a few whispers. When he got to the paragraph describing Charles's friendship with Jack Maguire, the silence became absolute.

He described the friends' meeting on Eagle Bluff, their discovery of Jennifer, Jack's insistence that he should be the one to go down for her, his calming words to the terrified girl, the struggle to the top, and the moment Charles wrapped Jennifer in his jacket.

"Jack did one more thing—he made Charles promise not to tell anyone that he'd seen him—at least not for a couple of days. Jack had been arrested for joyriding in a stolen car. He was supposed to be in court two days later, but he had decided to run away, even though Charles tried to talk him out of it.

"Charles kept his promise. Later, when he could have told the truth, he wasn't able to. He thought he'd be letting down people who believed in him. But he was so ashamed when people kept telling him he was a hero that he enlisted in the Army to get away. That's how he became a medic and saved people's lives."

Jerry looked up into a sea of shocked faces. Charles walked up to the microphone. Relieved to get offstage, Jerry slipped into an empty chair in the first row.

Charles adjusted the microphone to his height. "First of all, I'd like to commend Jerry on his fine report. You should know that I wasn't the one who first came forward with the real story. Jerry turned that up himself when he used his initiative and located Jennifer Atwood Martin in Westerfield.

"But when he'd heard her story, he gave me the chance to tell him what really happened.

"I've lived with this knowledge a long time—too long. For the sake of Jack Maguire and his family, I should have set the record straight years ago."

Jerry looked down the row. Danny's mother was looking into her lap. Tears ran down her face. Danny, looking embarrassed, patted her hand.

Charles cleared his throat and continued. "Even though my courage failed me then, I want everyone to know that there is no dishonesty in my service record. But, as I told Jerry, I know that my bravery under fire was fueled by my shame at not telling the truth when I should have. I wanted to live up to the name I'd been given. I wanted to be the hero that people here thought I was.

"Jack Maguire was the hero on Eagle Bluff. I've found out that Jack has had some difficult times since then, but nobody can ever take away what he did. I deeply regret that it's taken me until now to tell all of you. I apologize to his sister Kathleen Casey and his nephew Danny Casey."

Charles walked back to his seat. Scattered applause broke out, then more applause, and more—although Jerry saw people who weren't applauding. Suddenly the whole audience seemed to be in motion. Chairs were shoved aside. People pushed their way to the front of the room. A cluster of people gathered around Danny and his mother.

"We always knew Jack had good in him," said one woman.

"He'll surprise you yet," said another.

Danny's mother nodded, without looking up.

Jerry thought he should go over to them, but he didn't know what to say. He found himself surrounded by his classmates bombarding him with questions. His parents squeezed through the crowd.

"Well done, Jerry," said his father.

"So that's why you were asking about Charles having a tattoo," said his mother. "I wondered."

Jerry was surprised to see Nate.

"No way I'd miss this, Jerry."

Charles came over. Jerry's mother put an arm around his shoulder. "You'll never be anything but a hero to us, Charles."

"Thanks, Margaret. That means a lot to me." He put his hand out to Jerry. "This was the right thing to do, Jerry. I'm glad things worked out the way they did."

Jerry shook his hand. He wanted to shake Danny's, too, but Danny was still sitting with his mother, surrounded by her friends.

Regina Elliott elbowed her way to Charles. "You're aces in my book, Charles. Nothing changes that, not even that dreadful mall project of yours."

He laughed. "Regina, I'm glad to hear it."

"But," she continued, "we need to make a public acknowledgment of the facts you've made known to us. I'm thinking of the plaque. I'm calling a special meeting of the parks committee for tomorrow evening." She turned to Jerry's mother. "Your place. Seven-thirty sharp." She took out a notepad and pen. "Now, how do I get in touch with Mr. Maguire? May I assume from that tactful reference to 'difficult times' that he's in jail? I just overheard a remark to that effect."

"It's true," said Jerry. "I can find out from Danny exactly where he is."

"Let's find out together. You can introduce me." She took Jerry's hand and bulldozed through the group of people surrounding the Caseys.

"I appreciate this is an emotional moment, dear," Mrs. Elliott said when she'd been introduced to Danny's mother, "but I need some information from you and I'm overdue at my Friends of the Library meeting. If we're to give your brother public recognition, I need to know his proper name. Surely, it's John."

Danny's mother seemed dumbfounded by the tiny energetic woman who confronted her.

"No, it isn't. It's Jack. Just plain Jack."

Jerry looked around for Danny. He was standing a little distance away, talking to a white-haired man.

"And remember," the man was saying, "your uncle will be a free man one day. Well, good night, son." The man left.

Danny walked up to Jerry. "I thought your cousin was such a great guy with all those medals and everything. But he's been lying. And so were you. Why didn't you tell me about my uncle?"

"Not telling isn't the same thing as lying."

"Sometimes it is." Danny looked away. "So, was this some kind of big secret between you and your pals?"

"No, I didn't tell anybody. Except my cousin Nate. He was with me at Jennifer's house."

"You should have told me."

"I wasn't sure at first. When I found out for sure, Charles asked me not to tell anybody. He wanted to explain things himself."

"Lucky him. He gets a big audience. He gets anything he wants. When does my uncle get to do that?"

"I thought you'd be happy that I found out all this stuff."

"Okay, so maybe I am."

"Then why are you mad at me? I'm the one who's been your friend."

"You never wanted to be my friend. You'd pick your other friends over me in a second." Danny turned away and went back to his mother.

Jerry wanted to yell, You're wrong, that's not fair. But sometimes he didn't want to be Danny's friend. Danny made it too hard.

When Jerry saw his father wave to him and point to the door, he followed him out.

When they got home, Jerry's mother cut up the last of the banana cake and they all sat around the kitchen table.

"I turned thirteen a couple of weeks after Jennifer was rescued," Jerry's mother said. "I remember, at my birthday party, how withdrawn Charles was—not like himself at all. Everyone was shocked when he enlisted."

They talked a while longer, then she said, "I'm turning in. Jerry, we're proud of you." She patted his shoulder and went upstairs.

After a minute, Jerry's father said, "You and Danny seemed to be having some trouble. Care to talk about it?"

Jerry briefly described his problems with Danny.

"What do you think you should do about it?" said his father.

"I guess I have to talk to him. But I don't know what to say."

"Tell him what you've just told me. You have to figure out what you want and ask for it, Jerry. Otherwise, nothing will change."

"I know." But Jerry wondered if he'd get the chance to say anything to Danny now.

The next evening, Jerry passed around trays of tea and cookies to the five parks committee members sitting in the Wheelock living room. Regina Elliott consulted the clipboard in her lap.

"We have a happy coincidence here. July 25 is the anniversary of the rescue. That happens to fall on a Sunday this year. Wouldn't that be perfect for the installation of the new plaque?"

"That's a month from now," said Cynthia Gardiner. "Can we get a plaque that quickly?"

"I'll have a chat with the folks at the Leland Foundry. They've gotten so many jobs from the town, I'm sure they'll put a rush on it. All we have to do is give them the wording. Margaret, I'm putting you on the case. Can you come up with a rough draft by the next meeting?"

"I'll give it my best."

"Good. Now we should send an official notification to Mr. Maguire about the recognition he's getting. I'll write something tonight and get it in the mail."

"What will you say, Regina?" said Cynthia. "We can't exactly invite him to attend."

"I'll describe what's happened and explain about the new plaque. It's unfortunate that he'll be unable to attend, et cetera, et cetera, but his sister and his nephew can stand in for him, et cetera, et cetera." She shoved her clipboard into her satchel and reached for a cookie. "I think we have everything in hand."

Once Removed

Saturday morning, a week after the council meeting, the Wheelocks' doorbell rang. When Jerry answered it, Regina Elliott was standing there, holding an envelope.

"Is your mother in?" She marched past him into the kitchen without waiting for a reply.

Jerry's parents were at the table, still in their bathrobes, having coffee.

"Margaret, listen to this."

"I'll leave you two to chat," said Jerry's father, picking up his cup.

"Stay put, Cal." She pulled a letter out of the envelope and read it aloud. 'Dear Mrs. Elliott, I got your letter on Tuesday. Good news—I had a parole hearing on June 11 and the parole board has approved my release. I'm coming out in three weeks. I'll be staying with my sister Kathleen. So I'll be there when you put up that new plaque.' "

She put down the letter. "I did express the hope that we'd have a good turnout. This should absolutely guarantee one. Now all I have to do is write a diplomatic introduction. Curiously, the etiquette books don't cover situations like this."

"I'm sure you'll bring it off, Regina," said Jerry's mother. "You're a trouper."

"Coffee?" said Jerry's father.

"Thanks, Margaret, and yes, please, Cal. Black, no sugar."

"Does he say anything about where he's going to settle?" said Jerry's father.

"No, but I spoke to his sister this morning. He's going to live in Warren. Seems he had a legitimate job there once." Mrs. Elliott turned back to the letter. "There's something more you should hear: 'P.S. Charles is mistaken if he gives me all the credit. I don't think he realizes how close I was to total exhaustion the last few feet up Eagle Bluff. He used an emergency technique—as he took up the slack, he started rocking back and forth, using his body as a lever. That pulled us up the rest of the way.' "

"Mrs. Elliott," said Jerry, "may I have a copy of the letter? I want to show Danny."

"I don't see why not."

Jerry pedaled to Babcock's Quick Copy and back before Mrs. Elliott had finished her coffee. Then he biked to the Caseys'.

Danny was coming out the front door when Jerry turned down his block. They hadn't gotten together in the week since the awards ceremony, but now Danny ran to meet him.

"My uncle's got parole! My mom told me last night. We just got a letter from him. And he's going to stay with us, at least for a while."

"Your uncle sent Mrs. Elliott a letter, too." Jerry showed the photocopy to Danny, reading the P.S. out loud.

"I guess I was wrong about your cousin. I was steamed that night, but now everything's different. Hey, I have to go to the bakery for my mom. After we do that, we're on our own."

"Danny, we have to straighten out a couple of things."

"No, everything's fine now, like I say."

"The last time you saw me, you said that I lied to you and that I never wanted to be your friend."

"Oh, that. Forget it."

Danny's sudden happiness was like a barrier Jerry had to penetrate.

"Danny, I'm not going to the bakery or anyplace else right now. You know, sometimes I don't want to be your friend."

That hit home. Danny shoved his hands into his pockets and looked away. "I knew I was right."

"I said sometimes I don't. A lot of the time, we do really interesting things and then I want to be your friend. But you're always the boss. You never ask me what I want to do. You don't care. And you can't call somebody a liar and then take it back like it never happened. People have feelings, you know."

"I know. They're always after me about that in the program."

"Then why don't you listen?"

Danny shrugged. "I listen. I just forget the rest of the time."

"If we're going to be friends, you have to remember."

They stood in silence for a minute. Then Jerry said, "I want you to know, I didn't tell any of my friends anything I didn't tell you."

"You said that."

"I wasn't sure you believed me. But I've got other friends, Danny. I like them, too."

"I haven't."

Jerry didn't have an answer for that.

"So, do you want to go to the bakery?" Danny said.

"Sure. The Acropolis?"

Like magic, Danny's good mood was back. "No, it's another place, right near here."

For once, it was. When they got there, several people were in line. The woman in front of them turned around. "You're Danny Casey, aren't you?"

Danny nodded.

"Danny's uncle is the one who saved the little girl," she announced to the others.

"It's a great thing that the truth has come out," said the woman behind the counter. People nodded.

"My friend Jerry turned it up," said Danny.

A man gave Jerry the thumbs-up sign. Jerry

smiled back, but he felt strange. He felt that he should speak up for Charles, but he didn't know what to say. He wished the line would move faster.

A few minutes later, they left the bakery.

"You didn't tell them your uncle's getting out," said Jerry.

"They'll find out when he gets here. I want to see the looks on people's faces when they see him."

They passed a stationery store selling American flags.

"Hey, Danny, tomorrow's the Fourth of July. Want to meet me at Bennett Park for the parade?"

"Sure. What time?"

"Noon."

"I'll come as Paul Revere's horse. You can't miss me."

"Wait a minute," said Jerry. "Let's go in. I need to get something."

He bought a small package of envelopes. He took out the copy of Jack's letter, scribbled a greeting on it, slipped it into an envelope, and addressed it to Charles. Then he bought a stamp from the machine by the door.

"I want my cousin to see this," he said as he dropped the envelope into the postbox on the corner.

Jerry got to the park early on Sunday. He went to the bandstand to watch the preparations.

"Testing, testing," said a man into the microphone. Two girls in colonial costumes passed a mirror back and forth. A man dressed as Ben Franklin adjusted his spectacles.

"It's always an interesting sight—the Founding Fathers speaking into a microphone."

Jerry turned around. Charles was standing behind him.

"Of course," his cousin continued, "Ben Franklin loved new inventions. And Thomas Jefferson was a gadget freak. How're you doing, Jerry?"

"Great. You know, Danny's uncle is getting out on parole."

"Yes, Regina Elliott told me. Danny must be on cloud nine."

"Pretty much. I'm meeting him here in a few minutes."

Jerry was about to tell Charles what Jack had written in his letter. Then he decided that Charles should read it firsthand in Jack's own words.

A drum and bugle corps began rehearsing next to the bandstand.

"Jerry, I'll stake you to a hot dog. We should check them out before they've boiled for two hours."

"Too late," said Nate Farnsworth, who had come up behind them. "But then Fourth of July hot dogs are supposed to be boiled for two hours minimum, so they'll resemble the beef jerky our ancestors ate. It's patriotic."

"I love Fourth of July," he continued on the way to the hot-dog booth. "It's my annual opportunity to hear how the Farnsworths saved the Republic."

"To hear my dad's family, you'd think it was the Wheelocks," said Jerry.

"Forget it. It was the Findlays," said Charles.

A line was already forming at the hot-dog booth. The man tending it was laughing and joking with the two men at the head of the line. As Jerry, Nate, and Charles stepped up, Jerry noticed that the man's friendly expression disappeared. He nodded curtly when Charles gave their orders.

"Jerry," said Nate, "I've been meaning to tell you, you were a pro onstage."

"Thanks. I was really nervous."

Nate turned to Charles. "No regrets?"

"None. Do you know, this is the first Fourth of July since I was eighteen that I don't feel like hiding somewhere?"

Danny appeared on the other side of the park.

"Thanks for the hot dog, Charles. I've got to go. Bye, Nate. Thanks for all your help."

"Not at all. I'll send my bill in the morning."

As he walked across the field, Jerry thought about Charles's last remark. Maybe this was a different Fourth of July for Danny, too.

During the next week, Danny either talked non-stop about his uncle or didn't talk much at all, which wasn't like him. He seemed to need time to think.

Something else was different, too. Danny started asking Jerry if a plan was okay with him. Jerry could see the effort that took—sometimes Danny had to backtrack after taking charge in his usual way.

Meanwhile, Jerry was nervous about meeting Jack

Maguire. He imagined the scene and tried to think of the right things to say, remarks like the ones he heard on TV cop shows. He wondered if people would cry a lot. That would be embarrassing, but he'd promised Danny to be there at the bus station when his uncle arrived on Monday, July 12.

The day started out overcast, but by the time the bus pulled in at two in the afternoon the sun had come out. A young man was the first passenger to get off. He assisted the elderly woman behind him. A gray-haired man in a plaid shirt got off, then a teenaged girl. Two people were still getting luggage from the overhead racks. Danny fidgeted, his eyes riveted on the door of the bus. Then Jerry realized that the gray-haired man had stopped in front of Danny's mother.

"Hi, Kathy," he said.

"Hi, Jack."

The man patted her shoulder awkwardly. Then he ruffled Danny's hair. "Hi ya, kid."

Danny looked stunned.

The man stuck out his hand to Jerry. "Hi, I'm Jack Maguire."

"Jerry Wheelock." He tried to sound casual.

Danny was staring at his uncle. "Why isn't your hair black anymore?"

Jack laughed. "Well, I've been so busy, I missed my appointment at the beauty parlor."

Danny didn't seem to think that was funny.

His mother gestured toward the car. "We're parked over there."

Jack Maguire was only a little taller than his sister, but wiry, like Danny. Jerry couldn't decide if he was relieved or disappointed that Jack wasn't what he expected.

Jack got in the front passenger seat. In the back seat next to Jerry, Danny was silent.

As they drove down Bridgewater Avenue, Danny's uncle kept turning his head to look at both sides of the street.

"Kathy, could we stop and get an ice-cream cone from Marsh's? I've been dying for a Marsh's cone since . . . well, for a long time."

"Marsh's is gone. The place is a pizza parlor."

"Oh. Then let's get pizza. I'll bet these guys would like a pizza."

Two blocks farther on, they parked and went into Al's Speedy Pizza. Danny's uncle slipped on a pair of glasses to read the menu board behind the counter. Jerry noticed that the glasses were bifocals, like the ones his father had.

"How about one large with everything on it?" he said. His sister nodded. "How about you, Jerry?"

"Fine with me, Mr. Maguire."

"Call me Jack."

He gave the order and they found a table. While they waited, Jerry watched Jack. He wasn't like the movie tough guy Danny had described, but he wasn't like other people either. He was looking around like a tourist. At the same time, he seemed like somebody who knew a lot of things.

By the time the pizza arrived, Danny was his usual self again. In between bites, he asked his uncle questions about life in prison. Jerry wasn't sure if the answers were brief because Danny's uncle was trying to eat or because he didn't want to talk about it.

Danny reached for a second slice of pizza. "Show Jerry your tattoo, Uncle Jack. You know, that's how he figured the whole thing out."

Jack shifted in his seat.

"It's gone," he said at last. "I had it removed."

Danny's face fell. "When? Let's see."

His uncle rolled up his sleeve. A piece of gauze was taped to his forearm. He lifted the tape and flipped back the gauze. Jerry saw a patch of reddened skin.

"They let me out on Friday morning, Danny. I had it all arranged with a doctor in Warren. He took it off with a laser that afternoon. I stayed in Warren for the weekend so he could check that it was healing okay."

"Why did you do that?" said Danny, sounding like he was going to cry.

"It was a dumb thing to do in the first place, Danny. But that's all in the past." He put the gauze back and rolled down his sleeve.

After that, Danny didn't say anything.

"I remember the day I first saw that tattoo," said his mother. "I had just started grade school. I remember you coming in the door. Mom was so mad when she saw that thing."

Jack laughed. "She was a terror."

Danny's mother and uncle talked for a while longer about arrangements at the house. Then they all left the pizza place.

"I can drop you off at your house, Jerry," said Danny's mother.

"Thanks, Mrs. Casey."

Jerry was afraid to look at Danny on the way to the Wheelocks'. When they got there, he jumped out and waved to everybody. Then he remembered that he'd been invited to the Caseys' the next morning.

"See you tomorrow!" he yelled. Danny barely nodded.

Jerry was not looking forward to the visit.

Blackjack

As Jerry came up the Caseys' back steps the next morning, Blackie started to bark.

"Door's open," called Jack.

When Jerry walked in, Jack was sitting alone in the kitchen reading the paper. Jerry saw that it was open to the financial pages. His father read the financial pages.

Jack looked up. "I guess you're surprised. You see, a few years back, I got a new cellmate, Al Rogers. Al was a financial adviser. He couldn't keep his hand out of the till, but he knew a lot about making money the legal way. I listened to him and I figured out something real important—stealing is a lousy way to make money."

He turned the page. "I had some money saved up from the jobs I'd had in between my two prison stretches. I started picking up a few shares of stock here and there."

"While you were still . . ."

"Uh-huh. All you need to do is make a few phone calls."

He pointed to a stock listing. "This one's done okay for me." He turned the page again. "I'm thinking of getting into a mutual fund."

Jerry was aware that Danny had come down the stairs and was standing in the hall while Jack was talking. Now he walked into the kitchen.

"Mrs. Thompson across the street goes in for bingo. She figures she'll hit it big someday. Maybe you should try it. Sounds better than stocks. At least, when you lose, you see where the money went."

"Well, Danny, I gave up going for the big score. It costs too much."

Danny's mother came down the stairs.

"Hi, Jerry. Sorry I've got to run. I'm working a half-day today, so maybe I'll see you later. Danny, your room is a disaster. At least get the stuff off the floor."

"No can do. Jerry and I have plans for today."

Jack looked sharply at Danny, but he said nothing.

"I can't argue about it now," she said as she went out the door.

Jack sat back in his chair with a thoughtful expression on his face. From the driveway came the raspy sounds of an ignition that wouldn't catch. They all went out to see.

"Okay, Mr. Mechanic," said Danny's mother, "what's wrong with it?"

Jack raised the hood and began poking here and there in the engine.

"Are you a mechanic?" Jerry said.

"That's right. I don't just know how to steal these things—I know how to fix them, too."

He unscrewed the wing nuts that held the carburetor cover on.

"Look, Jack," said Danny's mother, "if this is going to take all morning, I'll call a cab."

"Give me a minute."

"Jack, I can't afford to be late." She got out of the car, slamming the door behind her.

"Take it easy, Kathy. Getting riled won't help."

"That's okay for you to say." She began pacing the driveway. "You know, you've had it pretty good these past eight years—a roof over your head, food on the table, nobody to support."

"It wasn't exactly paradise."

"No, I mean it." Her voice rose in anger. "You weren't around when Mom got sick. She was sick a whole year before she died. And when Dad had his heart attack, you were in prison then, too. Mom was so upset, she couldn't make the funeral arrangements. I was only nineteen, but I had to do it."

Jack tinkered with a spark plug. "Try it now, Kathy."

She slid in behind the wheel and turned the key. The engine started. Jack pulled down the hood and walked around to the side of the car.

"I didn't do what I did to hurt you, Kathy."

"But that's what happened all the same. I was only two years older than that little girl you saved. You rescued her. But you left me." She slammed the car door again, backed out of the driveway, and headed down Howell Street.

After a minute, Jack turned around. "Danny—"

Danny shrugged off the hand Jack tried to put on

his shoulder. "I think you should go live in Warren or wherever you're going. I think you should go right now." He sounded as if he might cry. "I've got to take Blackie for a walk. And I don't want anybody coming with me."

He pounded up the steps. Jerry heard the jingle of Blackie's leash. Then the front door banged shut. He and Jack were left standing in the driveway.

"Danny didn't mean that," said Jerry. "He talks about you all the time. He really looks up to you."

"Thanks, Jerry. But I'm afraid he's been admiring the wrong things." He went into the house.

Jerry sat down on the steps. He waited a half hour for Danny. Then he got his bike and pedaled home.

He let himself in with his key. Usually, he would go to his mother's shop if he came home before she did. The back room had a comfy chair for reading and an extra desk he could use. Just now, he wanted to be by himself to think. He flopped into an armchair.

After he'd read his report at the awards ceremony, he'd felt that he'd really done something good for Danny, especially when he'd seen the changes in him. But how much good had he done? Danny and his mother were both so angry. This wasn't the homecoming any of them had expected.

He flipped through a few magazines, not really reading anything. Then the phone rang. When he answered it, Jack was on the line.

"Jerry, I got your phone number off a piece of paper on the fridge. Is Danny with you?"

"No. Didn't he come back after he walked Blackie?"

"No. I'm worried. Do you have any idea where he might be?"

"I think so. It's in the woods near Miller's Creek. I'll have to show you. I'll be there in a few minutes."

When Jerry arrived at the Caseys', Jack was waiting in the driveway.

"I left a note for Danny if he comes back," he said.

Jerry put his bike in the garage, and they started off on foot. When they got to the clearing, Blackie bounded toward them, tail wagging. Danny was standing by the blind.

"You guys would never pass your Indian scout test. I heard you coming a mile away."

"Sit down, Danny," said Jack. "We need to talk. Jerry, you can hear this, too."

They sat.

"I don't blame you and your mother for being angry. I know a little about that myself. My father didn't leave like yours did, Danny, but he wasn't much of a father either. He was a hard man. Not so much to Kathy, but to me. I won't go into all that, but by the time I was your age I was one angry kid. All that hotshot stuff—dropping out of school, joyriding—that was me getting back at the world. Great way to get back. I got arrested for joyriding.

"After I ran away, I found out, you don't finish high school, you better like sweeping floors because that's the kind of job you'll get. If you're lucky. But I figured the world owed me and I was still trying to collect, so I started stealing cars for cash, not for joyrides. When I got arrested for that, I lost five years of my life."

Danny drew circles in the dirt with a twig.

"I came out, I was still angry. I swept a lot more floors. Yeah, I worked some better jobs, too. I was even a short-order cook for a while. Don't laugh. I

was good. But I could never stick with anything—
'cause, see, the world owed me.

"One day, I met somebody with a great idea. Hi-
jack an armored car and we'll be set up for the rest
of our lives. We had the whole thing planned. Well,
things didn't go that way. A guard got shot. He
nearly died, Danny."

Danny stopped drawing. "Did you shoot him?"

"Does it matter to you?"

"Yeah."

Jerry had a rush of thoughts. Somehow he knew
that Jack would tell the truth. Would it be what
Danny wanted to hear? Did he even know what
Danny wanted to hear?

"No, Danny, I didn't have the gun. I know everybody says that, but I didn't."

"Good," said Danny.

"But in court, that doesn't matter. I was in on the
robbery. I was as guilty as the guy who did it. That's
why I was in for eight years."

Blackie raced after a squirrel. It ran up a tree,
leaving Blackie whining at the base.

"I missed most of your growing up, Danny. That's
the worst of it. I should have been here."

Danny shrugged. "Everybody leaves."

"But I came back."

"You're going to live in Warren."

"Well, I've been thinking about that." Jack tossed an acorn for Blackie to chase. "So, what do you say, Danny? Do we go home?"

Danny toyed with a pebble. Then he nodded. "Come on, Blackie, that squirrel's in the next county by now."

"And one more thing," Jack said, as they started back to the trail. "I don't ever want to hear you talk back to your mother again. Got that?"

"Got it."

When they reached the trail, Jerry noticed that Jack kept scanning the ridge above them.

"Did you used to climb around here?" Jerry said.

Jack pointed. "I must have climbed every inch of that rockface."

When they walked up the Caseys' driveway, Danny's mother was unloading groceries from the car.

"We'll get that," said Jack, taking the bags she was carrying. "Kathy, is Connolly's Sporting Goods still in business?"

"The son runs it now. What are you looking for?"

"I thought I'd check out their climbing gear."

"Jack, there's boxes of that stuff in the attic."

"You kept it?"

"I kept it."

They hauled the boxes down to the living room.

"I've got things to do," Danny's mother said. She went to the kitchen.

Jack opened a box. "Look, Kathy, my freshman and sophomore yearbooks."

"If you'd finished, you'd have four of them," she said from the kitchen.

"I did finish. Got my GED a few years ago. I've taken some college courses, too."

She came to the doorway. "Jack, I didn't know. I guess that was my fault. I should have written."

"You had good reason to be fed up with me. I was fed up with myself. Especially after Mom died. I turned forty a couple of months after that. It really hit me what a waste my life had been. That's when I decided to make some changes." He reached in the box and pulled out a tool kit.

"Hey, this is from shop class."

Danny's mother sat down on the ottoman and

took the kit. "You made doll furniture for me with these tools. Do you remember? Beautiful little chairs and a table and a bed. I still have them."

"I remember."

Jack opened another box. He began pulling out coils of nylon rope, rubber-soled shoes, metal fastenings, a book on climbing.

"Charles gave me this," he said, opening up the book. "He's a great guy."

"So great that all these years he took the credit for what you did," said Danny's mother. "I'm sorry, Jerry, I know he's your cousin, but he should have told the truth before now. It's not like people have had such a high opinion of the Maguires all these years."

"Mom, I told you what Uncle Jack said about Charles helping at the end."

"I know, but that's the way I feel."

They took a break for lunch.

"So, Jack," Danny's mother said, passing around a plate of cold meat, "you're going to take up climbing again?"

"Think you're in shape for it?" Danny said with a mischievous grin.

"The prison had a fine gym. I'm in shape, all right. The question is, are you?"

Danny was caught by surprise. He didn't seem to know how to take Jack's question.

"Since you figure I'm over the hill," Jack continued, "I thought you might like to show me what a tough guy looks like."

Jack's tone was quiet, but unsettling. For the first time since he'd met him, Jerry realized that Blackjack was a good nickname for him.

"I'll bet Jerry would like to learn," said Jack. "Wouldn't you, Jerry?"

Jerry nodded. He didn't see what else he could do, even though the last thing in the world he wanted was to go climbing.

"And you'll come, won't you, Kathy?"

"Sure. Somebody's got to tell 'em where to find the bodies."

"I'll come," Danny said. "When?"

"How about tomorrow if the weather's good?"

"You're on."

Jerry's heart sank.

After lunch, Jack took Danny and Jerry to Connolly's Sporting Goods to buy new ropes. He looked over the displays of the latest climbing gear as if he'd just arrived from another planet. "You could climb a glass wall with these shoes. That's okay—sneakers are fine for now. And you can wear your bicycle helmets."

Back at the Caseys', they practiced knots until late that afternoon. Jerry phoned home after he was invited to dinner.

"Ask them about going climbing," Danny said. "Uncle Jack says you've got to have permission or it's no go."

Jerry saw his last chance for a reprieve.

"Dad, Jack's taking Danny and his mother rock climbing tomorrow. They want me to go. I won't if you think I shouldn't. Because it's too dangerous."

"Did you say Danny's mother is going along?"

"Yes."

"Are you going to wear some kind of helmet?"

"My bike helmet."

"Well, Jack knows his climbing, whatever else he's done. Okay. You can go."

Rats, thought Jerry.

At dinner, he tried to sound enthusiastic for the next day's adventure. Danny clearly was. They talked until seven-thirty. Danny's mother looked at her watch.

"Jerry, it's late. Throw your bike in the trunk and I'll give you a lift home. Danny, you'd better take Blackie for a walk."

On the way to the Wheelocks', Danny's mother said, "I'm glad I have a chance to talk to you alone, Jerry. Danny doesn't know this—and I'd rather not tell him just now—but I knew about Jack's getting parole a week before the awards ceremony. He phoned me. When he told me he was going to live in Warren, I said, fine. I wasn't even going to tell Danny that his uncle was out, not right away. I've been afraid of Danny's trying to imitate him—like stealing the comic books. And I was angry. Then I heard your report. I wrote to Jack that night and asked him to come stay with us, at least until he got on his feet. Now I see how much he's changed."

She pulled up in front of the Wheelocks'. "So I wanted to thank you."

"Thanks for telling me, Mrs. Casey. I won't say anything to Danny."

Jerry got his bicycle out of the trunk and waved goodbye.

Learning the Ropes

On the drive to Eagle Bluff the next morning, Danny was as excited as Jerry had ever seen him.

"Are we going to the place where you rescued the girl?"

"Near there."

They parked at the trailhead. Jack opened the trunk and hauled out a bag of equipment and two coils of nylon rope.

"Remember," he said, as he handed a coil to Jerry and one to Danny, "your rope is your lifeline. Treat it with respect. Don't ever drag it when you don't have to, don't step on it, don't snag it on sharp rocks. And if you fall three times with the rope catching you, buy a new rope."

Jerry didn't like the sound of that last point.

A few hundred yards down the trail, they reached the fork. Going left would have taken them to the top of the bluff. Jack went right.

"Aren't we going the wrong way?" Danny said.

Jack didn't answer.

After a short distance, they broke out of the woods. From that point, the trail skirted the bluff rising on their left. On their right, a stand of low trees blocked the view of Miller's Creek.

Jack stopped at a level spot on the trail.

"This isn't where you were that time," said Danny.

Jack pointed straight up. "See that ledge to the left of the clump of bushes? I rappelled down to there. That's about two hundred feet up."

Jerry shaded his eyes as he picked out the spot. "Are we going up there?"

Jack laughed. "Maybe someday. Today we're staying a lot closer to terra firma."

"We're not going to just mess around on some boulders, are we?" said Danny. "I've done that lots of times."

"I guess that explains the scraped elbows and knees," said his mother.

"Oh," said Jack, seemingly slow to understand, "you mean you've done bouldering." He slung down the bag he was carrying and approached the rockface. "Let's see . . . how did we use to do that?"

He planted the toe of his left sneaker on a ledge and slid his right hand into a crevice. The next thing Jerry knew, Jack was moving directly sideways three feet off the ground, like a fly crawling over a plaster wall.

With movements as graceful as a dancer's, he went about thirty feet to the right, then started back to the left.

"Wow," said Danny. "He's Spider-Man."

Jack got back to his starting point and stepped lightly onto the ground. "Is that what you meant?" Jerry was sure Jack was holding back a smile.

"Can you teach me how to do that?" said Danny.

"Put on your helmet," said his mother. "You haven't got any brains to waste."

"Very funny," said Danny. But he eagerly strapped on his bicycle helmet.

"Let's move down a ways," said Jack. "The cliff isn't so steep there."

They walked about fifty feet down the trail.

"Now listen up," said Jack. "Your feet and legs are a lot stronger than your hands and arms. Climb with your feet whenever you can. Use your hands for balance." He put his finger on a narrow ledge. "Here's a good toehold."

"I don't think it's wide enough, Uncle Jack."

"It's plenty wide," said Jack, hoisting Danny up. "Get your toe on it. That's it. I won't let you fall. Now look around. Do you see a handhold?"

Danny looked around. "No."

"Sure?"

"There's no handhold, Uncle Jack," Danny said, his voice rising.

"What about that crevice?" said Jack. "Think you can slip your hand in there?"

"I don't know . . . Okay, I got it. Now what?"

"Make a fist. See how that holds you? That's called jamming. There are lots of different jams you can do with your hands and your feet."

"I see another crevice."

"Great. Use it."

Jack talked Danny through move after move.

Jerry began to see that the rockface wasn't featureless after all. It was full of ridges and cracks that became handholds and toeholds—if you knew what you were doing.

Jack knew what he was doing, and Danny was figuring it out fast. Jerry could see that. Once he was over the first unfamiliar moves, he eagerly followed every suggestion Jack gave him, besides working out new holds for himself.

And Jerry could see how happy Jack was to have such an apt pupil.

"Hey, Danny," said Jack, "it's time to give Jerry a turn."

Reluctantly, Danny jumped the short distance to the ground.

"It's fun, Jerry," he said, pulling off his helmet. "You don't have to worry about falling."

Jerry put on his helmet.

As Jack helped him to his first foothold, he said, "Everybody has his own style of climbing, Jerry. You have to find what works for you."

What worked for him, Jerry thought, was keeping his feet on solid ground. He saw a crevice and slipped his hand into it.

"That's it," said Jack. "Remember what worked for other climbers and use it."

To Jerry's surprise, forcing his fist against the sides of the crevice held him as well as any regular handhold. He scraped his toe over the rock, feeling for a second foothold.

Jack guided Jerry's foot to a ledge. Jerry slid his hand along until it slipped into a crevice. This one was too small for a fist.

"Jam with your fingers," said Jack.

As Jack coached him along, Jerry began to feel that maybe he could do this. He'd never be like Jack or Danny, but maybe he wasn't the world's biggest klutz. He scraped his hands over and over. Some of the scrapes even bled a little, but he didn't care. His mind was on the next move.

When he had gotten about half as far as Danny had, Jack said, "You did terrific, Jerry, but I think we need a break."

Jerry jumped down. Only then did he realize that he was trembling from the strain. His legs wobbled. Jack had made it look so easy.

Danny's mother took a turn. Even Danny was surprised at how strong she was.

"Okay," she said, after getting almost as far as Jerry, "that's enough for one day. I'm going back to being expedition photographer."

"Danny," said Jack, "ready to try again?"

"Aren't we going to do some climbing?" said Danny. "You know, there's a direction we haven't tried. It's called 'up.' "

"I don't think you're ready for it, Danny," said Jack. "What I showed you just now is only a tiny part of what you need to know."

"Can't we rig up safety ropes so we don't get hurt?"

Jack looked at his sister. She shrugged her shoulders. "Maybe he should try it, Jack. At least I won't have to listen to him complain all week."

"Okay," said Jack. He began walking along the trail, leaning back to search the rockface.

"What are you looking for, Uncle Jack?"

"A place where there's an easy way up—right next to a hard way up." He stopped. "There. Danny, bring me my bag."

Jack pulled out a palm-sized metal wedge with a loop hanging from it. "Jerry, find me a carabiner."

Jerry was pleased that he was able to pick one out from the heap of metal gear in the bag.

Jack snapped the D-shaped carabiner onto the loop and clipped the whole assembly to his belt. Then he coiled the rope and slung it over his shoulder.

"Now I get to take the easy way up." He grinned, putting on his helmet.

Once again, Jack scaled the bluff as if he had adhesive on his hands and feet.

When he was about twenty feet up, he stopped on a ledge and reached over to a crevice. He ran his hand up and down the thin opening, exploring it. Then he slipped the wedge into the widest part of the crevice and yanked down hard on the dangling carabiner. The wedge dropped a couple of inches, then stuck.

Jack uncoiled the rope and threaded one end through the carabiner until the rope was doubled back on itself. Grasping the doubled rope in both hands, he suspended himself from the wedge.

"That'll hold," he said.

He scrambled back onto the ledge, slipped the

rope under one leg and tossed it over the opposite shoulder. With his hands on the rope above and below him, he casually proceeded to stride backwards down the cliff in giant steps.

"Thought I'd take the elevator down," he said to his astonished audience. "I'm getting to be an old man." He rummaged around in his bag.

"Okay, Danny, put on the helmet and I'll rig up a harness for you. You're going to do what we call 'fixed rope' climbing. That means your harness will be tied to one end of the rope that's threaded through that carabiner up there. I'll be on the ground holding the other end. As you climb, I'll be taking up the slack. That way, you can't fall more than a couple of inches, as long as you don't climb higher than the carabiner."

Like everything else that Jack had done that morning, the rigging of the harness was smooth and efficient.

"The rope is only for protection, Danny. Don't use it as a handhold. Your hands are for balance."

"I get it. Can we start?"

Jack tugged the last of the knots tight. "Okay, kid,

now you get to take the hard way up. Stay to the left of that bulge in the rock."

The first part of the climb wasn't as steep as the place where they'd done the bouldering. Danny moved up the cliff with only a few pointers from Jack. About ten feet up, the angle got steeper. Jerry could see Danny starting to struggle. Farther up, the wall was nearly vertical.

"You're going to want to lean in toward the rock," called Jack. "Don't do it. Keep your weight over your feet."

Many seconds elapsed now between moves. Jerry could tell that Danny was scared, but he wouldn't quit. As he slid his right foot toward a ledge, Jack called, "Lean out, Danny. You're leaning in too much. You're going to slide."

"I can't lean out," Danny called back. His voice was sharp with fear. He seemed unable to move in any direction.

"That's okay," said Jack. "Remember—you can't fall. The rope will catch you. Can you back down?"

Danny started to ease his foot back. Then slid—fast. He slid only a couple of inches before the rope caught him, just like Jack said. But Jerry and Danny's mother both gasped.

"I've got you, Danny," called Jack. "I'm going to let you down slowly. Hold the rope with both hands and walk backwards if you can. Otherwise, just let yourself slide down."

Jack let out the rope until Danny was back on the ground.

"That was tougher than I thought," Danny said. His hands shook as he tried to unfasten his harness.

"You did real well, Danny," said Jack. "With practice, you'll get the hang of balancing." He quickly undid the knots on the harness. "Any other takers? Kathy?"

"No, thanks."

"I'd like to try it," Jerry said. The words seemed to be coming from somebody else.

"Take my advice and stop when it gets too hard," said Danny.

When Jerry had his harness on, Jack said, "Remember what I said before. Watch the climber ahead of you. See what worked for him—and don't repeat his mistakes."

Jerry found a foothold and started up the cliff.

Using his newfound knowledge, he made slow but steady upward progress.

As the climb got steeper, he made a deal with himself. He'd take one more step, then ask Jack to take him down the way he had done with Danny. After he took the step, he made the same deal over again.

He heard shutter snaps.

"You're doing great, Jerry," said Danny's mother.

Jerry wanted to thank her for the encouragement, but he didn't dare. He was afraid the effort of speaking would destroy what little balance he had.

"Don't look at the ground, Jerry. Look at the rock in front of you," said Jack. "Imagine you're two inches off the ground."

But he wasn't two inches off the ground and no amount of imagining could distract him from the fear that was settling over him like a cloak. Jerry couldn't figure it out. Some place deep in his brain refused to believe in the safety rope. It kept insisting that this climb was life or death. Every move became a battle.

By the time he got to the steepest section, he was tired of making deals with himself. His arms and legs felt as if they were turning into jelly. He risked a glance upward. Only about three feet more and he'd reach the wedge that held his safety rope.

"Don't lean in."

Jack's voice seemed to come from the inside of Jerry's head instead of twenty feet below him. He slid his foot to a new hold. Don't lean in. With his eyes closed, he ran his hand along the rock until it slipped into a crevice. Using a fist jam, he gained a few more inches. He found a ledge, then another and another. Don't lean in.

"No farther, Jerry," called Jack. "You're at the top."

"Jerry, you made it!" yelled Danny. His mother was snapping pictures.

Jerry opened his eyes. The rock was only inches in front of his face. He mustn't turn. He must keep facing forward. Behind him, he could hear birdcalls and the rapids just past the bend in the creek. He might never have another chance like this. He turned around.

He was above the trees. He could see Miller's Creek, and beyond that the emerald-green alfalfa fields of Brown's Farm, dotted with ponds, the out-skirts of town where tidy frame houses stood in rows, and beyond that, the towers and steeples of the town center. He'd seen it all from the top of Eagle Bluff, but the view had never been so beauti-ful before, a wondrous quilt that rolled before him, spreading to the gray-blue horizon.

The following Saturday morning, a manila enve-lope arrived with the Wheelocks' mail.

"It's from the Caseys," said Jerry's mother as she walked back into the kitchen. She slid the contents, two pieces of cardboard rubber-banded together, onto the table. A handwritten note was clipped to the cardboard: "What do you think of Jerry? Yours, Kathleen & Danny."

His mother separated the cardboard sandwich. "Jerry, it's a picture of you."

It had been taken just as he turned around at the top of his climb.

Before he could get a good look at it, his mother was carrying it into the living room. She took a frame off the mantel and shook out the photo-graph.

"Great-uncle Edgar will have to step aside until I can get another frame. I need this one."

She slipped in the photograph of Jerry and replaced the frame on the mantel.

"Much better," she said.

Heroes

On the last Sunday in July, the crowd began gathering on Eagle Bluff before noon, although the installation ceremony wasn't set to begin until one.

A rope barrier had been put up to keep people away from the edge. The new plaque was covered with a blue silk cloth. A microphone stood nearby.

As Jerry kept a lookout for Danny, a steady stream of Findlays, Wheelocks, and Farnsworths came up the path, as well as school friends and neighbors, but a lot of the people arriving were strangers to Jerry.

Newcomers blended into the crowd, and the mingled conversations made the clearing sound like one cheerful Tower of Babel. Just after twelve-thirty, Danny and his mother arrived with Jack.

Once again, Jerry couldn't reach Danny because of the people that encircled the Caseys. After a minute, he felt a tap on his shoulder.

"Hi, Jer. Did you climb up or take the easy way?"

"Hi, Danny. How did you get behind me?"

"I sneaked past the sentries and outflanked your troops. Where's your cousin?"

"He isn't here yet."

"I think he called my uncle yesterday. I was out for a walk with Blackie. When I got back, my mom said something to Uncle Jack about how he must have called out of guilt."

Across the clearing, Danny's mother waved to them.

"Come on," said Danny. "Say hello."

As Jerry walked up to the Caseys, Jack turned to him with a smile, but he seemed nervous.

"It's the big day," he said.

"It certainly is."

In the awkward silence that followed, Jerry heard someone say in a low voice, "That's his cousin."

Jerry told himself that the comment was a simple statement of fact, but he began to feel uneasy. He scanned the crowd to see if Charles had arrived.

A ripple of movement passed through the group around Jack. A petite figure emerged from the crush.

"Jack Maguire, I presume. Regina Elliott." She pumped his hand. "Terrific to see you here. We should be starting right on time. Got your speech?"

Jack stuck his hand into his breast pocket. A look of fear, then relief crossed his face. "I've got it." He sounded like one of Jerry's classmates who'd just found his missing homework. There was no one like Mrs. Elliott.

"Good. See you in a bit." She disappeared into the crowd.

Jack unfolded the piece of paper he'd taken out of his pocket. He glanced over the lines of handwriting on it. "I wrote this up last night. I hope it's okay."

"Jack, it's fine," said Danny's mother, putting a hand on his arm. "Don't worry."

On the other side of the clearing, where his parents were standing, Jerry heard voices and saw people looking toward the path. Charles had arrived.

From behind him, Jerry heard someone say, "There's Mr. Success, the big war hero."

Danny was some distance away, talking to an elderly man, but Jerry knew that Jack had heard the remarks. Their eyes met for a second. Jack looked as uncomfortable as Jerry felt.

Mrs. Elliott walked over to Charles and shook his hand. Other people did the same, or slapped him on the back. Laughter erupted from the group every few seconds. Meanwhile, the people where Jerry stood had become mostly silent, watching the greetings.

Danny's uncle was watching, too. Jerry sensed that Jack was about to walk over to Charles, but, as he began to move in that direction, Mrs. Elliott started tapping the microphone to test it.

"Good afternoon, everyone. I think we can begin this afternoon's ceremony. Thank you all for coming. First, I'd like to introduce our mayor, Bob Easton, who will say a few words."

Jerry didn't pay much attention to the mayor's

speech. His mind was on Charles. He was worried. Would the people he'd overheard make remarks when Charles was speaking?

Jerry waited impatiently through two more speeches. Mrs. Elliott stepped up to the microphone.

"Now I want to introduce the man you've all been waiting to hear. As a very young man, Jack Maguire took a great risk to save the life of a little girl. Mr. Maguire, will you please come forward?"

Jack approached the microphone. He unfolded the paper in his hand, put on his glasses, and started to read in a flat, quiet voice.

"I am truly honored by the plaque that's being dedicated today. It's something I'll always be able to point to with pride. I hope it will be an inspiration . . ."

Jack stopped. "This isn't what I want to say." He folded the paper into a pocket and took off his glasses.

"I've heard remarks around town and I heard some more here today. I think I need to set a few things straight.

"Some people have been talking about how Charles should have told the truth. But what about me? Shouldn't I have faced up to what I'd done? Stealing the car for a joyride, I mean. If I had, my whole life might have been different. But I made my choice.

"I want you to ask yourselves—what difference would it have made if Charles had told the truth after I didn't show up for my court date? What I know is, by the next morning I was halfway across the country.

"So, what would have happened? For one thing, Charles wouldn't have gone to Vietnam and saved the lives of those men.

"But, for me, would the truth coming out years ago have made a difference? I don't know. I never will know. All I know is, it makes a difference to me now."

Jack searched the crowd. "Charles, will you come up here?"

As Charles stepped forward, Jack described the levering technique Charles had used to pull him and Jennifer the last few feet to safety.

"With half a dozen feet to go, I was nearly spent. All the willpower in the world won't help you once that happens.

"But there's a more important point. When I got to Eagle Bluff that day, I had one thought in my head—getting away. If I'd been alone, would I have stopped to see who was crying? Or would I have figured it was just an animal? But I wasn't alone, I was with Charles. He was there looking for a lost child. What really saved Jennifer was Charles's instinct to put himself on the line for a stranger.

"The story's here," said Jack, folding back the silk covering on the plaque, "and this is the truth."

In the silence that followed, Danny's mother walked up to the microphone.

"When I was six, I thought my older brother knew everything. Later on, I figured out that he didn't. But after what he just said, I realize that he knows what he's talking about here." She turned to Charles and put out her hand. With a look of pleased surprise, he took it.

Applause began. It spread in all directions until Jerry couldn't see anyone who wasn't applauding.

He wasn't sure what would happen after the ceremony, but at this moment everyone there was on the same side.

Danny came up to shake Charles's hand. Jerry started to walk over to them, when someone called his name. He turned around. Jennifer Martin was there, with her baby on her hip. When he'd invited her to come, she hadn't been sure she could attend.

"Isn't this wonderful, Jerry? I'm so glad I came. I feel as if a weight's been lifted off me. Isn't it funny? My parents moved us away to escape the memories, but all the years since I've been carrying a burden and I didn't even know it."

Jennifer shifted the baby and waved to Regina Elliott, who was waving and pointing to the microphone. "I think Mrs. Elliott wants to introduce us."

Jerry hung back. "You go."

"You come, too. This all happened because you found me. Don't you feel that you've really done something?"

Jerry looked around. "I guess I do."

The baby suddenly gave a squeal and waved tiny fists in the air.

"Is that a girl?" said Jerry.

"Yes."

"What's her name?"

"Charlene. I named her after Charles. Her middle name is Mary, but I'm thinking of changing it to Jacqueline, after Jack Maguire. Charlene Jacqueline. What do you think?"

Jerry thought it sounded fine.